Forbidden Desires

Forbidden Desires

Marina Anderson

www.xratedbooks.co.uk

An *X Libris* Book

First published by X Libris in 1996
Reprinted 2000, 2004

Copyright © Marina Anderson 1996

The moral right of the author has been asserted.

A CIP catalogue record for this book
is available from the British Library.

ISBN 0 7515 1730 5

Photoset in North Wales by
Derek Doyle & Associates, Mold, Clwyd
Printed and bound in Great Britain by
Clays Ltd, St Ives plc

X Libris
An imprint of
Time Warner Book Group UK
Brettenham House
Lancaster Place
London WC2E 7EN

Forbidden Desires

Chapter One

HARRIET SAT IN the back of the limousine, her long legs crossed, and stared out of the window at the relentless driving rain. This wasn't the Cornwall of her childhood memories. Then the sun had always shone and she'd spent hours on the rugged beaches surfing and sunbathing. She shivered and Lewis put his arm round her.

'Cold, or nervous?' he asked with a smile.

'Inappropriately dressed,' said Harriet ruefully. Certainly her lemon-yellow short-sleeved linen jacket worn over a soft floral print skirt with a matching scarf round her neck were inappropriate for the English weather, but that wasn't the truth, and both she and Lewis knew it.

'You like Edmund and Noella, don't you?' he queried.

'Of course I do; Edmund's one of those intriguing men who make you want to get to know them better, and Noella is so open and enthusiastic it's impossible to dislike her.'

'She's certainly enthusiastic. I'm relieved we're driving down in separate cars. I don't think I could have coped with her constant little screams of appreciation at everything English on a journey of this length.'

'I hadn't realised how many hours it would take,' sighed Harriet, snuggling up closer to her husband of less than two days. 'We've been travelling for nearly twelve hours now.'

'We've got six weeks to recuperate,' he reminded her. 'Is that too long for a honeymoon, do you think?' he added teasingly.

Harriet turned to him, her grey eyes solemn. 'But this isn't just a honeymoon, is it?'

He shrugged, the smile still playing around his mouth, a mouth that Harriet was suddenly overwhelmed with a desire to kiss. She pushed the thought away, waiting for him to answer her. He didn't.

'Is it, Lewis?' she repeated.

'I'm going to do some work as well,' he admitted. 'That's why Mark's coming along, although he won't be joining us for a couple of days yet.'

'Which means we've really got a two-day honeymoon!'

Lewis touched her gently on the cheek, his long fingers caressing her with exquisite tenderness. 'Do you honestly think we need a honeymoon?'

Harriet smiled, remembering the countless times they'd made love since their first meeting

2

over two years earlier when she'd gone to work for his first wife, the famous film star Rowena Farmer. 'I suppose not,' she agreed.

'Besides, you enjoy the excitement of making a film with me,' he reminded her, his hand moving to rest on her exposed knee.

'Last time I didn't know I was making a film,' she pointed out.

'Isn't it even more exciting knowing from the start?'

This was a question Harriet had been asking herself during the long flight from America. When she'd met Lewis James he'd just begun working on his first *cinéma vérité* film, *Dark Secret*. She'd been chosen to join his London household for the duration of their stay there, as an unwitting player in the script he was writing as real life events actually unfolded; events of such electric eroticism that the film, when it was made, had become the biggest hit of the year.

Now, finally married to Lewis, Harriet was once again to star in the sequel *Forbidden Desires*. The difference this time was that she knew she was being placed in a situation designed by Lewis, and that her reactions and those of the other players in the as yet unscripted plot would determine the film's outcome.

'Well?' he whispered, his breath warm against her ear.

Her physical hunger for him, her almost desperate need to feel their bodies pressed together and his hands and lips on her flesh, threatened to overwhelm her. 'I don't know,' she said with total honesty. 'It rather depends on what the plot is about.'

'Exactly what the title suggests, Harriet, forbidden desires.'

'Whose forbidden desires?' she murmured as his mouth travelled down the side of her face.

'Yours, Edmund's and Noella's of course.'

'What about you? Don't you have any forbidden desires?'

'Not at this moment,' he replied evenly. 'Right now my sole desire is to make love to you, and since you're my wife that's allowed.'

'I don't want anyone else either,' she whispered, turning her face towards him and letting his light kisses move closer to her mouth.

'That's all right then, you've nothing to worry about, have you?'

'But you won't have a film!' she exclaimed, pulling back from him just as their lips were about to meet.

Lewis looked thoughtfully at her. 'Harriet, trust me. No one can resist forbidden fruit. Sooner or later you'll be tempted.'

'And you don't mind?' she asked in astonishment.

'This film isn't about what I mind or don't mind. It will reflect what happens when a man is so much in love with his wife that he allows her to do anything that makes her happy.'

'Anything at all?'

'Yes, anything at all,' he repeated.

'And suppose that you find yourself attracted to forbidden fruit as well?'

'We'll just have to wait and see, won't we?'

'I don't want you falling in love with anyone else,' complained Harriet. 'We've only just got married!'

'We're not talking about love, Harriet. We're talking about sexual desire. Don't worry, everything will be all right. Besides, I don't want you getting bored.'

'How can I be bored after two days of marriage?' asked Harriet in bewilderment.

'You didn't want to get married,' Lewis reminded her. 'I had to persuade you, and your chief argument against it was fear of boredom, remember?'

'Yes,' she agreed, 'but . . .'

'No buts, Harriet. I'm simply making sure you don't feel trapped.'

'You want me to make love with Edmund during this holiday, don't you?' she said accusingly.

'I don't *want* you to do anything at all. I simply want to see what happens during the course of the next six weeks, and to that end I've tried to make sure we spend plenty of time with interesting people.'

'What if nothing happens and we don't get on?'

'End of film plan! It won't matter. I've plenty of other ideas up my sleeve.'

'But Edmund's putting up money for *Forbidden Desires*, he'll want results.'

Lewis smiled. 'Edmund desires *you*, that's why he'll want results!'

A faint flicker of something perilously close to desire darted through Harriet. She knew that Lewis was telling the truth; she'd felt Edmund's desire the moment they met straight after the wedding, and she knew deep down that it would be easy to have an affair with him. There was, as she'd already admitted to Lewis, something intriguingly enigmatic about him.

'What if it all goes wrong?' she repeated. 'Suppose you and I fall out of love?'

'Then the film won't have a very high feel-good factor! Stop worrying, Harriet, you must have faith in me. I know what I'm doing.'

Harriet leant her head against his shoulder and closed her eyes to blot out the rain. She did trust him, but she had a terrible feeling that he'd probably said the same thing to Rowena at the start of *Dark Secret*, and that had ended with the disintegration of Rowena's marriage and the end of her career as an international film star.

'Your work means more to you than personal relationships,' she muttered as she drifted off to sleep.

Lewis didn't reply, he had a suspicion Harriet might be right.

Travelling behind them in the back of an equally comfortable limousine, Edmund Mitchell and his wife of ten years, Noella, were also discussing the forthcoming holiday. However, unlike Harriet and Lewis, they were unaware of the roles in which Lewis had cast them or the importance of their behaviour to the plot of his forthcoming film.

'Isn't it just great?' enthused Noella for at least the twentieth time on what seemed to Edmund to be an interminable drive.

'Isn't what great?' he asked quietly, refusing to allow his irritation to show.

'The rain, honey. I mean, this is why English women have such great complexions. None of that dried-out prune look for them, it's all peaches and cream and the natural scrubbed look.'

'Naturally drowned more like,' retorted Edmund. 'You seem to forget, Noella, that I was born here. In fact, I've spent over half my life in the complexion-enhancing dampness of the English climate, and right now I wish I was back home in Beverly Hills.'

Noella ran her fingers lightly up his right thigh. 'Don't get grouchy, not before we've even started the holiday, sweetie. You've always told me you adored Cornwall.'

'Not when it was wet, and I haven't always told you any such thing. I may have mentioned once or twice that America lacked a similar coastline but that was all.'

Noella smiled to herself. She adored the way Edmund insisted on getting every detail right. His refusal to exaggerate or over-dramatise events was one of his greatest attractions to her, second only to his extraordinary expertise in bed. Remembering their most recent bout of lovemaking,

7

which had occurred only a few hours after Lewis and Harriet had finally tied the knot, she wriggled slightly on the leather seat.

If anything, Edmund had shown extra finesse that night, prolonging the session into the small hours of the morning until even Noella had been exhausted. Yet – and here she forced herself to admit a rather unpalatable truth – despite her final sense of satiation, the almost dangerous sophistication of some of the things they'd engaged in that night had more than once brought with them a feeling of nearly unbearable frustration.

Edmund liked to prolong everything, to refuse her that final pleasure until he'd explored every possible avenue of enhancement, and really Noella was a woman who liked her sex to be raunchy, physical and fierce. She wished that just once in a while Edmund would take her without any of the endless preliminaries or rules that now dominated their sexual life.

Immediately she realised where her thoughts were leading and put a stop to them. She knew very well that she was lucky to be married to Edmund. Educated at Eton, he'd made his money on the stock market at an early age and now, when he'd just passed his fortieth birthday, he liked to use part of his considerable fortune to back films and plays that would otherwise never be seen. A powerful figure behind the scenes in the world of the performing arts, Edmund was admired and respected, and this meant that

Noella was admired and respected too, something that a girl with her start in life could never have imagined happening.

In any case, no other man had ever kept her so satisfied sexually. Even if their tastes were beginning to diverge, he was still easily the best lover she'd ever had and she was determined to keep the marriage intact. As his third wife she was well aware that this might not be easy, but she held a lot of weapons in her armoury.

Edmund liked a woman with strong appetites, and he liked Noella's voluptuous figure and the strikingly sexy clothes she wore to accentuate it. After ten years of marriage he could still be aroused by the sight of her slipping on a tight-fitting black dress, putting on huge gold ear-rings and bracelets, and then going out with her, knowing that beneath it she was naked. With her blonde hair piled on top of her head and her glamorous make-up always in place even before they took breakfast on their patio, she was the epitome of the sexy blonde wife so beloved by straight-laced Englishmen in their dreams; only Edmund had made the dream a reality and Noella intended to keep him satisfied in every possible way.

'How much further, honey?' she asked, running a hand through his short, curly brown hair.

Edmund glanced at his watch. 'Another half hour or so, I think. Why don't you have a nap? We've been travelling for hours now and you

9

don't want to be half dead when we arrive.'

Noella leant back against the cushioned upholstery and closed her eyes. She certainly didn't want to be tired when they arrived at Penruan House, and since Edmund was clearly disinclined to talk she decided to take up his suggestion.

As his wife drifted off to sleep, Edmund Mitchell stared out at the driving rain and, just as Harriet had earlier, wondered why it was that things were always so different from the way you remembered them. It must have rained before during some of his trips to Cornwall, but those days had vanished in his memory while the sunny times had remained as vivid images that encapsulated some of the happiest days of his life.

He heard Noella's breathing slow and even out and realised that she was asleep. Giving a small sigh of relief he allowed himself to relax and settled into his corner of the back seat. Unknown to her, Edmund was beginning to tire of Noella. All his adult life he'd been searching for the perfect partner, someone intelligent, witty and sensuous, who would share in all his interests, both sexual and cerebral, but so far this combination had eluded him.

Noella had seemed close to what he wanted and for a long time he'd been reasonably content, but after ten years he was starting to realise that he was never going to smooth out her rough edges. They had once seemed endearing but were now nothing but an irritation. Her claims to connections with the world of performing arts had also been revealed as less than strictly accurate. In Edmund's view, two years as a striptease dancer in a less than salubrious nightclub in New Orleans was hardly a claim to artistic fame. Not that Noella knew he'd discovered her secret, and he had no intention of mentioning it to her because it would be unfair. He'd married her knowing that she was probably not all that she claimed but her vibrant sexuality and vivid good looks had seemed ample compensation. Now they weren't, and he had the suspicion that he was beginning to disappoint Noella as well.

Even so, he'd been content to continue as he was until that moment, only two days ago, when he'd first set eyes on Harriet. He'd known then that he had to have her, had to possess her and discover whether she was the one he was looking for, the perfect partner to enhance his life.

He thought that Lewis was aware of this but for some extraordinary reason didn't seem to mind – in fact this shared holiday had been Lewis's idea. Edmund wasn't going to think too deeply about the reasons behind this. He had always been a man who took his chances where he could, and if Lewis was going to offer him a chance of Harriet, however remote, then he'd take it.

He liked Lewis, admired his work and was happy to back it, but that wasn't going to prevent him from trying to take Harriet away from him if he wanted her badly enough. Desire, thought

Edmund as the car purred along through the drizzle, was a powerful spur and showed a callous disregard for moral principles. The fact that Harriet was just married and therefore should be regarded as strictly out of bounds only made his desire all the sharper. Forbidden fruits, as he knew very well, had the sweetest taste of all.

By the time Harriet and Lewis finally arrived at Penruan House the rain had eased and was little more than a fine mist. Stepping from the car Harriet realised with relief that here at least it was warm, damp yes, but at least the bone-chilling cold of London had vanished.

Lewis stretched his legs and glanced about him, his eyes taking in the large Elizabethan-style house built of grey stone and covered with trailing ivy, flanked by long sweeps of lawn stretching away on either side. He noticed too the outdoor pool and hoped the weather would improve sufficiently for them to use it, and smiled when he saw that the grounds also housed a small pitch-and-putt course. He knew that Edmund could never resist a bet, and so far Edmund had failed to beat him at anything connected with sport. He rather relished the idea of beating him on a regular basis on this small course, and wondered vaguely why it was that he should want to beat him so badly.

'At least it's warm,' enthused Harriet, already picturing the house and grounds in bright sunlight rather than the soft mist.

Lewis raised an eyebrow. 'Warm? How fortunate we didn't come here in mid-winter!'

'Well, it isn't cold, is it?' she laughed, her eyes shining.

Looking at her, her face alight with happiness, Lewis thought how lucky he was that she'd agreed to marry him. He knew without any doubt at all that if he were to lose her he would be heartbroken. For a moment a chill touched the back of his neck and he felt goosebumps rise on his forearms.

Before he could reply Edmund and Noella's car arrived. Noella was the first out, her tight red skirt rising to the middle of her thighs as she stepped on to the drive.

'How cute!' she squealed, glancing around her. 'Edmund, honey, just take a look at this place. It's like something out of a fairy story!'

Edmund came round from his side of the car and stood beside his wife, one hand resting lightly on her shoulder. Immaculate as ever, in a three-piece navy suit, crisp white shirt and maroon silk tie, he looked more like a barrister or surgeon than a film backer, and Harriet, seeing him and his tall, blatantly sexual, blonde wife standing together, wondered what on earth they could have in common apart from the sex.

Edmund's soft dark eyes met hers and for a moment she had the terrible feeling that he could read her mind because there was a slight smile playing at the corners of his sensuous mouth.

'How's the blushing bride?' he asked laconically.

'Exhausted!' retorted Harriet.

13

'And the bridegroom?'

Lewis grinned. 'Tired, but not too tired. Let's hope the rain stops soon. I'm anxious to see all these views that Harriet's been on about.'

Lewis's chauffeur cleared his throat. 'Forecast's good, sir,' he ventured. 'I've got a cousin lives near here. He told me it was going to be hot and dry for the next three weeks.'

'No doubt he tells all the visitors that!' laughed Lewis. 'Get the cases inside, please. We've stood out in this rain long enough. Come on, darling,' he added, putting an arm round Harriet's waist. 'There's meant to be a housekeeper on call, let's hope she's got the kettle on.'

'I'm dying for a cup of tea,' agreed Harriet.

Edmund watched the two of them walking into the house, studied the movement of Harriet's legs through the flimsy material of her skirt, and felt a flutter of excitement behind his ribs. He'd seen the way she'd looked at him when he'd been standing with Noella, and read the look in her eyes. Clearly she was intrigued by him, and that was very much to his advantage.

'I'm freezing,' complained Noella. 'Why didn't I bring my fur wrap?'

'Because it's midsummer and you didn't think you'd need it. Anyway, a fur wrap would be a little out of place here. I'll warm you up later,' he promised, his eyes suddenly narrowing.

'Let's take a bath together,' suggested Noella as they entered the lobby. 'I'll let you soap my back if you let me—'

Before she could finish a young man of about twenty-eight came out of one of the doors that led into the lobby and held out his hand. 'Mr James? I'm Oliver Kesby, the owner of Penruan House. I hope everything's as you requested, but if you should find—'

'I'm not Mr James,' interrupted Edmund. 'He's already inside. I'm Edmund Mitchell and this is my wife Noella. We're staying here with Lewis.'

Oliver's tanned face coloured and he hesitated, unsure how to proceed.

Noella studied him with interest. He was around five feet ten inches tall and very well built. His thick dark brown hair was cut quite short which emphasised the almost perfect shape of his head, while his eyes, which were light blue with dark lashes, were positively magnetic.

'You mean this is your home?' she exclaimed. 'Gee, if it were my home I sure as hell wouldn't let it out to other people in the summertime.'

Oliver shifted his weight from one foot to the other. 'It's a matter of finance really,' he murmured. 'Besides, this place is far too big for me. I've got a nice cottage in the grounds. I live there all through the letting season.'

'How interesting,' said Edmund, his voice clearly indicating that it wasn't.

Oliver blushed even more fiercely. 'Perhaps you could tell Mr James where to find me if he needs anything,' he suggested awkwardly.

'Perhaps I could,' agreed Edmund. 'The question is, *will* I?'

15

'Ignore him, he loves to be pedantic,' Noella told the bewildered Oliver, before hurrying her husband through the entrance lobby into the main hall.

'You weren't very nice to him, Edmund,' she said reproachfully, as soon as they were out of Oliver's earshot.

'You more than made up for that,' said Edmund curtly. 'I thought you were going to eat him up on the spot.'

The door to the drawing room opened and Harriet put her head out. 'Come and look at this, you two, it's really lovely. And Mrs Webster's making us some tea and scones, and—'

'You like the simple pleasures of life, do you, Harriet?' asked Edmund softly.

Harriet stopped what she was saying and turned a surprisingly cool gaze on her husband's friend. 'Yes, as a matter of fact I do. Is there anything wrong with that?'

He smiled, and when he did so his whole face changed. It became more open and added some much needed warmth to his presence. 'Nothing at all,' he assured her. 'In fact, it should mean that you thoroughly appreciate our landlord, Oliver Kesby.'

'I take it that means you think he's simple,' laughed Lewis, appearing in the doorway behind his wife.

Noella walked into the drawing room, pushing past the newlyweds and leaving her husband in the hall. 'He's gone on the turn,' she announced to no one in particular. 'Just ignore him; with any luck his mood might change in an hour or two.'

Lewis looked questioningly at Edmund. 'Anything wrong?'

Edmund shook his head. 'Of course not, everything's fine. I'm feeling a trifle jet lagged, that's all.'

'Come and sit in here; that should make you feel better. There's even a genuine log fire, unlit but still very reassuring.'

'You're a lucky man, Lewis,' Edmund murmured beneath his breath as he walked past his friend. 'For the first time ever, I really envy you.'

This was exactly the kind of thing Lewis had hoped to hear from the point of view of his script. After all, he knew that unless Edmund desired Harriet nothing would happen. Harriet wasn't the kind of person who would make the first move, especially on her honeymoon, but just the same he felt a sudden surge of anger that he had to struggle to suppress.

'What's that?' he asked in mock innocence. 'My fame?'

'Your wife,' said Edmund shortly, and even Lewis was taken aback by the strength of the emotion behind the two words.

'I've always had a weak spot for Noella,' Lewis retorted softly, but Edmund merely smiled. He knew full well that Noella wasn't Lewis's kind of woman. In fact, until the arrival of Harriet on the scene, Edmund had thought that Lewis would never allow himself to become deeply involved with any kind of woman. News of Lewis's impending second marriage had taken Edmund by surprise, but having met Harriet he fully understood Lewis's desire to make her his. The only thing was, Edmund suspected that Harriet was the kind of woman who never truly belonged to anyone.

The large drawing room was bright and cheerful. None of the furniture matched, but the overall effect was pleasing on the eye. Edmund sat down on a red two-seater sofa with a table lamp next to it and a profusion of red and black scatter cushions littered along the seat. He had to throw them on the floor before he could make himself comfortable.

Noella sat next to him, her almost matching red skirt again riding high up her thighs, while Harriet seated herself in a deep chair with a steeply angled back. She curled her long slim legs up beneath her in order to be comfortable. She was showing far less leg than Noella but the effect on both Edmund and Lewis was much greater.

As Mrs Webster brought in the tray of tea and scones and fussed around putting cups and plates on different tables, Lewis stood by one of the windows and watched the scene as dispassionately as he could.

It would transfer well to film he thought, and mentally tried to cast Noella from among the current list of popular blonde stars of the screen. Not too difficult he decided, and his eyes moved on to Harriet. The actress who'd played her in

Dark Secret had now married and retired to live in seclusion with some Italian prince, which meant the part would have to be recast and that would be difficult. Blatant sexuality was easy to play, the almost hidden enigmatic sexuality of Harriet was far harder to define and even more difficult to portray.

Edmund would be relatively easy. Well-spoken Brits were all the rage in Hollywood at the moment, and he could think of two straight off who would manage the part very well. They wouldn't mind the fact that the film's content would be so powerfully sexual because of the 'artistic' praise lavished on *Dark Secret*. An art film was always acceptable, he thought wryly.

His gaze lingered on Harriet who was listening to something Noella was saying and laughing with delight, her lips parted and her cheeks tinged with pink. He could so easily picture her naked, mentally strip her of her clothes and imagine her body beneath his, her head turning from side to side as her passion mounted. The vision was so real that he felt himself harden and quickly turned away from them all to stare out over the acres of garden.

Noella had finished talking now and, as Edmund began to tell a story to Harriet, she looked over to where Lewis was standing. Noella had always found his tall, dark good looks incredibly sexy, and could never look at his golden brown hands without wondering what they'd feel like on her body. She knew that she was of little interest to him. It was a pity because she felt sure they'd go well together, but desire was something you couldn't force, it was either there or it wasn't, and she would have bet all the money she had on the fact that as far as she was concerned, Lewis felt no desire at all.

But with regard to Harriet it was clearly a very different story. Noella remembered the way Lewis had behaved when he'd been married to Rowena, and it wasn't at all the way he was behaving around Harriet. Then, despite the fact that he was married to an international sex symbol, he'd seemed distant and detached. He'd been a challenge to almost every woman he met, but always remote. With Harriet he made his feelings plain. He was forever touching her or making eye contact. She thought that for the first time ever he felt a sense of antagonism towards Edmund, although she couldn't imagine why, since it was highly unlikely that even Edmund would initiate an affair with the new wife of America's hottest film director, especially when he was putting up the money for Lewis's next project and hoping to make a fortune from it.

In any case, it was Lewis who'd suggested they all spend the holiday together which, now that she'd seen him with Harriet, was very strange indeed. Honeymoons were meant for two people, not four, even when the bride and groom had been living together for over two years prior to the wedding. She wondered exactly what was going on.

'Aren't you having any tea?' Harriet asked Lewis, suddenly aware that he wasn't taking part in the general chatter.

'Sure, pour me a cup, will you? I'm just looking at the view,' he said distantly.

Harriet placed a cup for him on the table by her chair and a few minutes later he came and sat at her feet. Without thinking, she let one hand drop onto his head and, very slowly, lightly massaged his scalp with her fingers. With a sigh of contentment, Lewis let his head fall back against her knees and his left hand caress her ankle, the fingers encircling the bones in a soft rhythmic movement.

Noella smiled to herself and glanced at Edmund. To her surprise, he was staring at the newlyweds with a look of sexual hunger on his face. When he realised that she was looking at him, he turned to her and his face became expressionless again, but for that one brief moment she'd seen naked desire in his eyes and fear touched her.

'How about taking that bath we talked about earlier?' she suggested brightly.

'You go first,' said Edmund with a polite smile. 'I can wait a while. I'd rather like to eat another scone before I move off this sofa.'

'I can wait,' replied Noella.

'No, you go ahead,' insisted Edmund. 'I know how badly you feel the cold.'

'Hey, we were going to bath together, remember?' said Noella angrily.

21

Harriet's hand stopped moving over Lewis's scalp and she looked at Noella and Edmund in surprise. Lewis simply laughed and continued stroking his wife's ankle.

Edmund shrugged at Harriet's expression. 'What can I say? Noella's a very impatient woman!'

'And a lucky one!' laughed Harriet, anxious to dispel any momentary awkwardness.

As soon as she'd spoken, Lewis's hand stilled and he too looked across at Edmund, waiting to hear his friend's reply.

'I don't think I can really answer that,' said Edmund in an amused tone of voice. 'If I say yes it sounds like boasting and if I say no then—'

'Harriet will lose interest!' interrupted Lewis.

Harriet laughed, but Noella didn't. 'Come on, Eddie,' she said, trying to disguise her irritation.

Edmund's breath caught in his throat. 'Don't call me that, Noella, you know I hate it,' he said sharply.

'Yeah, well, I hate being kept waiting, you know that, too.' With a sigh Edmund got up from the sofa and followed his wife from the room.

Alone together, Harriet continued to caress her husband's head and neck, but although Lewis stroked her leg and even let his hand wander up inside her skirt to the soft flesh of her inner thigh, there was a warning bell sounding inside his head. He'd imagined that Edmund and Noella had a sound marriage. If he'd been wrong then he might very well have set up a far more dangerous scenario than he'd intended.

Chapter Two

LEWIS SAT AT the head of the table in the dining room that evening and wished that he wasn't always viewing life through the lens of a camera. No matter how many times he told himself that he'd take part in a social gathering rather than view it as an outsider, he ended up simply watching it, and tonight was no exception.

He decided that Harriet's 40s-style dress with its fitted waist, capped sleeves and padded shoulders, would have to go for the film. The colour was fine, primrose-yellow with grey dots, and the detailed lacing down the front was extremely sexy, but the long flared panels of the skirt would need to be shortened and thin shoulder straps would replace the padded coat-hanger look.

As for Noella, her brilliant scarlet silk jacket worn over a floral printed skirt and tunic top, both patterned with huge red roses, was too overwhelming for close-ups. It was fine seen from a distance, and it suited her, but the outfit would have to be more restrained if it was to work effectively on the large screen. He was trying to work out what colour he'd use instead when Harriet spoke.

'Is there something wrong, Lewis?' she asked mildly.

He blinked and tried to clear his thoughts. 'Wrong?'

'You keep staring at us, first Noella and then me.'

'I'm sorry, I was miles away,' he said with one of his quick stomach-turning smiles. Noella immediately forgave him; in any case, she was used to Edmund drifting off into his own world at meal times, but Harriet was less easily appeased. She guessed what Lewis was doing, and the fact that he was doing it on the first night of their honeymoon was infuriating.

Deciding to pay him back she turned and smiled at Edmund. 'Isn't the room lovely?' she said softly. 'It's so relaxing.'

Edmund, who had been pricing the cost of the dark carved-oak chairs and table along with the bright yellow and blue curtains suspended from a sturdy wooden pole by heavy oak rings, nodded thoughtfully. 'I suppose it is. It's certainly a peaceful place here. We could be the survivors of some nuclear war for all the signs of other human habitation. Actually I was admiring the collection of china over there. They must have set Oliver back a few pence.'

'Who's Oliver?' enquired Harriet.

Edmund glanced across the table at his wife. 'Perhaps you should really ask Noella. She paid him more attention than I did.'

'Oliver Kesby is our landlord,' said Noella shortly. 'Edmund mentioned him earlier, don't you remember?'

'Sorry, I must have been thinking about something else at the time,' admitted Harriet.

'That's because you haven't seen him,' said Edmund with a half-smile. 'He's what Noella always calls "a hunk".'

'He's just a nice looking young man,' retorted Noella, who had been in a less than cheerful mood ever since coming down to dinner. Harriet assumed that her bath-time had turned out to be less enjoyable than she'd anticipated.

'I must keep my eye out for him then,' Harriet said brightly.

'I'm sure you won't have any need of Oliver Kesby,' said Edmund, turning to look directly into Harriet's eyes. 'As I remember, Lewis has the reputation of keeping his women more than satisfied – until he tires of them, that is!'

'I can't imagine who told you that,' said Lewis, suddenly very alert with all thought of film direction banished from his mind.

'I have my spies.' Edmund sounded amused, as though he knew that he'd annoyed Lewis.

'I'm sure I won't *need* him,' agreed Harriet, 'but there's no harm in keeping something in reserve.

After all, Lewis intends to work for some of the time. When he's working I might want to play!'

'If you need someone to play with, promise you'll tell me before you start involving Oliver?' queried Edmund, putting a hand on Harriet's bare arm.

She smiled at him. 'I don't honestly think it's very likely, but yes, I promise.'

Lewis, who had leant forward to hear the words, was distracted at the last moment by Mrs Webster placing a huge bowl of lasagne in front of him, so he missed what was said and instead simply saw the picture of fleeting intimacy as Edmund's hand touched his wife's arm and her smiling directly at him, her eyes shining with either amusement or admiration.

'That looks great,' enthused Noella.

Mrs Webster smiled. 'One of my specials. I'm famous for my lasagnes, and my shepherds' pies, as Mr Kesby can vouch for only too well. Now, I'll fetch the green salad and then leave you all to help yourselves. There are desserts in the kitchen on the worktop. I usually leave about now, if that's all right with you, sir?' she added, looking at Lewis.

He nodded, his mind miles away. 'Of course, anything you like,' he murmured.

'You shouldn't say that,' Noella told him, once Mrs Webster had left the room. 'Next thing you know she'll be going off home in the middle of the afternoon.'

Lewis frowned. 'I shouldn't say what?'

'That she can do anything she likes.'

Lewis sighed. 'Don't you see, Noella, I have to say that, otherwise I might lose her.'

Noella frowned. 'Lose Mrs Webster?'

Lewis's dark eyes turned even darker and his mouth tightened. 'I wasn't talking about Mrs Webster.'

'No,' said Noella softly. 'I've just realised that.'

After they'd begun to eat, an awkward silence descended. For once Noella's bubbly chatter seemed to have deserted her, and Lewis seemed to be brooding on something, while Edmund, never particularly talkative, was always quite happy to remain silent.

Feeling slightly desperate, Harriet decided to try to draw Noella out a little. 'I've never heard the name Noella before,' she remarked. 'Is it common in your part of America?'

'Do you mean in strip clubs?' enquired Edmund smoothly.

Noella flashed him a look of puzzled annoyance. 'It's not my real name, honey,' she replied. 'I was christened Ella. It seems I was a real handful because my parents were forever having to say "no" to me, so much so that the first time I was asked what my name was I said it was "No-Ella" and it seemed to stick.'

Harriet laughed. 'That's a wonderful story.'

'The whole of Noella's life's a wonderful story,' said Edmund.

Lewis felt another twinge of unease. He'd never known Edmund and Noella bicker publicly with each other, and it seemed to him that it was

27

Edmund causing most of the trouble. He wished that he'd taken the trouble to check out the state of the Mitchells' marriage before he'd set up this scenario, but it was too late to change the cast now.

'Did you see the pitch-and-putt course, Edmund?' asked Lewis, deciding it was time he tried to smooth things over a little.

Edmund nodded. 'Going to try and take some money off me, are you?'

'As long as you haven't been having golf lessons behind my back, yes.'

'I don't do anything behind your back,' said Edmund.

Lewis tried to smile, knowing that he must encourage rather than discourage the situation that was already developing. 'I'm glad to hear it. I must say, I thought the grounds looked wonderful. Hopefully the sun will shine enough for you girls to use the pool.'

'I suppose Oliver services it,' said Harriet.

'He'll probably service anything we ask him to,' retorted Edmund. 'What do you think, Noella?'

His wife smiled over-brightly at him. 'I reckon you're right, honey. I certainly intend to make sure we get full value for money while we're here.'

'She's more careful with your money than she is with mine,' complained Edmund, but he smiled as he spoke. Harriet wasn't sure if the remark was meant to be taken seriously or not.

Listening to the other couple, Lewis suddenly

didñ't care. He'd finished his lasagne, had no desire for a dessert and no desire for coffee. All that he wanted now was to take Harriet upstairs and consummate their marriage.

To everyone's surprise including his own, he stood up, nearly tipping his chair over in his haste. 'I'm sure you two won't mind if Harriet and I go up now,' he said, his eyes smoky with desire. Noella felt her stomach turn over as she thought of the kind of night that lay ahead for Harriet.

'No coffee?' asked Edmund in mock-surprise.

'Not here; if I drink anything it's going to be champagne in the bedroom.'

'But what will you drink it from?' continued Edmund, his gaze challenging. 'A glass, or something more exciting?'

'Definitely not a glass. Harriet, what do you say?'

Harriet hadn't yet finished her lasagne, but she wasn't hungry for food, and hadn't been when the meal began. Like Lewis she was suddenly consumed with need and, blushing very slightly, she too pushed her chair back from the table. 'It has been a long day,' she admitted.

'No doubt it will be matched with a long night,' murmured Edmund beneath his breath. Harriet heard him, but she didn't acknowledge the words. At that moment all that interested her was Lewis.

'Well,' exclaimed Noella as the couple left the room, 'I guess that's what being newly married does for you. It sure beats being told to take a bath on my own.'

'Don't worry,' said Edmund, 'I'll make it up to you later.'

'She's cute, isn't she – Harriet, I mean,' said Noella.

Edmund nodded. 'She's very cute, she's also very intelligent and extremely good company. All in all I'd say she's more than Lewis deserves.'

'Really? Why do you say that?' enquired Noella, moving towards the door as she went to fetch their desserts.

'You know Lewis, he's too selfish. For him fiction is always more interesting than fact. Who else would have let Rowena Farmer slip through their fingers?'

'I was never sure she did slip, honey,' replied Noella, placing a bowl of strawberries and a pot of clotted cream in front of him. 'I had the feeling she was dropped by those capable-looking hands.'

'Still a very strange thing to do; although I suppose Harriet might persuade a man to do strange things.'

'She isn't nearly as beautiful as Rowena,' retorted Noella, looking longingly at the cream but then remembering her already ample curves.

'She's far more sensual,' said Edmund, dipping one of the strawberries into the cream, lifting it to his mouth and slowly biting off the end with even, white teeth.

'How do you know?'

'A man can tell these things. Rowena was a sex goddess, Harriet's real. I can imagine her. . .' His voice tailed off as he put the rest of the strawberry into his mouth.

'Imagine her doing what?' asked Noella sharply.

Edmund gave a soft sigh of pleasure. 'All kinds of things,' he murmured.

Suddenly Noella's eyes brightened. 'Do you think she might be interested in joining us?' she asked eagerly.

Edmund smiled at her. 'You'd like that, wouldn't you? I remember the film starlet in Cannes; we had some fun that year, didn't we?'

'But would Harriet be interested?'

'I'm not sure,' admitted Edmund. 'She might take some persuading.'

Noella nodded. Knowing that Edmund was very interested in Lewis's new wife, and having no desire to lose him to her, she'd decided that the best solution was to encourage him, providing she was involved as well. 'Why not try and persuade her, then?' she suggested. 'If she likes you enough, maybe she'll be happy to follow your suggestions.'

'That sounds like a very good idea,' agreed Edmund, his mind already picturing the moment when he and Harriet would become lovers. 'So good that I think it deserves a reward.'

Noella felt her pulse rate increase and she moistened her lips with the tip of her tongue. 'Do I get to choose the reward?'

Edmund shook his head. 'I choose, but you're guaranteed satisfaction.'

Noella had to be content with that.

As Noella and Edmund discussed their plans, Harriet was standing on the polished pine floor of their bedroom, the backs of her thighs resting against the side of their king-size wrought-iron white bed, while Lewis slowly began to unlace the bodice of her dress.

The room was light and spacious with beautifully framed prints on the walls and vases of sweet-smelling flowers on each of the highly polished bedside tables, but Harriet didn't notice the decor, she was totally focused on Lewis and the expression of hunger in his eyes as his hands moved to undress her.

At last the dress was peeled off her shoulders and Harriet stepped out of it, leaving it in a crumpled heap at her feet. While Lewis unfastened the clip at the front of her lacy white bra, Harriet started to unbutton his shirt, her fingers clumsy in her haste.

'Slow down,' whispered Lewis. 'We've got the whole night ahead of us.'

Harriet knew that, but she still couldn't slow down. Her desire for him was rising rapidly, and when she felt her breasts freed from the constraints of the bra she made a tiny sound of pleasure. Her fingers worked quickly, until at last she was able to open up his shirt and move forward to press her aching breasts against his chest.

As she rubbed herself against him, Lewis felt her nipples hardening. He stroked her long brown hair, running his fingers through its golden streaks and pushing it back off her face, his fingers brushing her scalp in a soothing regular rhythm.

Harriet closed her eyes to savour the sensations. Next his hands moved to her back, caressing between her shoulder blades and then her shoulders and down the sides of her arms until all her skin started to tingle and with a soft moan she thrust her pelvis forward. Lewis shifted position until his right thigh was between her legs and Harriet pressed her pubic bone hard against it, so that gradually the lower half of her body started to come to life as well.

Lewis had managed to remove all of his clothes now, but Harriet was still wearing her french knickers. She felt his large hands slide inside the wide legs of her panties until he was grasping her buttocks, and his fingers softly squeezed and released the imprisoned flesh, sending sweet darts of pleasure through her lower belly.

Drawing back a little, Lewis lowered his head and moved his mouth down over her shoulders and across the hollows at the base of her neck before finally allowing his lips to touch her breasts.

Guiding her on to the bed, Lewis positioned himself by her side, and as her breathing quickened, he flicked his tongue across each of her erect nipples in turn, his mouth hard against the sensitive buds of pleasure. Harriet began to squirm with rising delight and wrapped her arms round his shoulders, her finger nails lightly scratching over his back.

When her nipples were tight and fully extended, Lewis drew the left one into his mouth and sucked steadily, increasing Harriet's excitement so that she twisted the lower half of her body towards him as an ache of desire started between her thighs.

Lewis continued to suck on each of her nipples until the tracing of veins on her breasts became more marked and the breasts themselves started to swell, a sign that she was well on the way to full arousal.

Harriet wished that he had more than one mouth, that his tongue and lips could travel over her body at the same time as he sucked and licked at her nipples. For one brief moment she imagined what it would be like if Edmund were there too, providing this additional excitement. Shocked at her thoughts, she pushed the image away into her subconscious but knew it would return at a later date.

Now Lewis's hands were travelling over her body, stroking the sides of her waist and her softly rounded belly, until at last she felt his long fingers brush almost imperceptibly across the opening of her vagina before moving on to her inner thighs.

Harriet didn't want him caressing her thighs, she wanted him back between her legs, touching her where she most needed it and where the previously sweet ache was starting to become painful in its intensity. She moved her legs restlessly but Lewis's only response was to graze the tip of one nipple with his teeth so that a jolt of electricity seemed to sear through her upper body.

At last his hands moved back to her vagina and once more he brushed over her entrance. His fingers carefully parted her silky pubic hair so that he could slide the pads of his fingers up and down her moist inner channel. The rhythm was quick but light and now Harriet's excitement began to reach fever pitch. The areolae around her nipples started to swell and Lewis included this area when his tongue swept over the surface of her breasts.

Harriet's breathing was quick and shallow as she felt her whole body clamouring for a climax. She moaned with desire, and hearing that sound Lewis finally allowed his fingertips to rub gently on each side of her clitoral shaft. Immediately a wonderful warmth started to suffuse Harriet's lower belly and her muscles tightened in preparation for the release of orgasm.

She was very moist and slippery; after a few minutes Lewis allowed the middle finger of his right hand to slide into her vagina while his thumb and forefinger continued to stimulate the entire clitoral area. His finger moved in and out, slowly at first but then more quickly, and all the time the clitoris was continuing to receive the kind of stimulation Harriet liked best.

Her body felt heavy and swollen with need, and

behind her clitoris she felt the first tingles of approaching orgasm. Her breath snagged in her throat and Lewis immediately eased his index finger into her vagina along with his middle finger and then drummed softly with his fingertips against her G-spot.

All the time he was caressing her between her thighs his mouth was continuing to play with her breasts, and suddenly he saw the tell-tale red flush start to appear on Harriet's chest and throat, which meant that she was rapidly approaching the point of no return.

'Are you close, Harriet?' he whispered, his fingers still massaging at the exquisitely sensitive G-spot.

Harriet could only mutter an unintelligible reply as her head moved back and forth against the bedspread.

'Tell me,' he insisted, suddenly slowing the pace of his caress.

'Yes! Yes!' shouted Harriet, terrified that he was going to stop or lose the rhythm that was leading so inexorably to the explosion she was longing for.

'I want you to come now,' he murmured, as his fingers moved inside her.

She was almost there now, her whole body taut and straining for the moment when the pleasure would flood through it, and her cries grew in urgency and strength. Lewis, aware that Edmund and Noella were in the adjoining room, took extra pleasure from the sounds and just as Harriet felt that she'd burst if she didn't climax, he nipped at the tender flesh of her left breast and this proved to be the trigger for her ultimate moment of pleasure.

Red hot currents of ecstasy streaked through her body. Her limbs went rigid while her toes curled upwards and with one final shout of delight her body exploded.

As the last tremors began to die away, Lewis positioned himself above her, his hands either side of her body, arms fully extended, and thrusted into her. Harriet lifted her legs and wrapped them tightly round his waist so that her pelvic area was stimulated by his thrustings; almost immediately she felt the blissful tightness start up again between her thighs.

Aware of her re-arousal Lewis slowed his pace, allowing her time to build to another climax and then as he felt her internal muscles start to contract around him, he let his body take over and the tempo of his thrusts increase once more. It didn't matter because Harriet was almost there.

'If only Edmund could see you now,' whispered Lewis, his dark eyes staring down into her grey ones with an unfathomable expression. His words sent her toppling over into another shattering climax and Lewis finally allowed himself to lose control, his hips pumping almost desperately as he triumphantly spilled his seed into his new wife.

Lying on top of the gold bedspread in the yellow bedroom, both Noella and Edmund could, as Lewis had guessed, hear Harriet's cries of passion only too well. Propped up on a pile of cushions, Edmund appeared to have all his attention focused on the blue and yellow floral print curtains. He was so still that he could have been asleep, but Noella knew that he wasn't. For one thing he had a huge erection, and his testicles were drawn tightly up at the base of his penis. His breathing, however, remained slow and even, and never by a single word or movement did he give any indication of his rising excitement.

For Noella, lying naked beside him, it was both annoying and arousing. Annoying because she wanted Edmund to be making love to her, but arousing because she was able to imagine Harriet uttering the same sounds in this room rather than the one she was sharing with Lewis. Noella could picture the other woman writhing beneath Edmund's skilful ministrations while she, Noella, held her down or added to the excitement by touching her softly and cleverly in the places Edmund left free.

After Harriet's second orgasm there was silence for a time, until at last Edmund moved, turning his head towards his wife. 'The honeymooners are certainly enjoying themselves,' he remarked dryly.

'I seem to remember being promised some enjoyment myself this evening,' Noella reminded him.

'I hadn't forgotten,' Edmund assured her. 'Open my small brown case there, there are one or two things I'll need.'

Uncertain whether to be pleased or not, Noella obeyed. Inside the case, lying on top of various items of clothes and ingenious gadgets, there was a sheepskin cover which she knew very well. Edmund got up off the bed and Noella spread it across the yellow bedspread, already anticipating the soft caress of the wool against her skin.

'Now put on the black leather halter-top outfit,' Edmund instructed her. For a moment she hesitated, but then without a word she drew it out and held it up to examine. 'Put it on,' repeated Edmund.

'I'm not sure how it goes,' complained Noella.

With a barely restrained sigh of impatience Edmund helped her into it, and Noella was swiftly clad in a shiny black leather suit that had virtually no top to it. The bottom half had a zip running from her belly-button down to her hip bones and a totally open crotch. Below her ample breasts the leather ended with a metal ring from which two wide straps spread upwards in a V-shape that went over her shoulders and joined at the back of her neck. A thong divided her back into two halves right down to where it joined up with the bottom half, just above the curves of her buttocks.

Thrust slightly upwards and totally exposed, her breasts jutted out proudly and Edmund eyed them with appreciation, his normally tight mouth relaxing in anticipation of the delights the night held for them both.

'You look fantastic!' he assured her as she turned round for him to inspect her. 'Take a look at yourself in the wardrobe mirror.'

Noella did, and automatically thrust her shoulders back to make her breasts stand out even more. Between her thighs she was already becoming damp.

Edmund reached down, ran his fingers along her opening and smiled. 'You're as eager as I am,' he said. 'That's good. Now lie on the sheepskin cover. Spread yourself out on your back, arms and legs extended in the shape of an X.'

'Are you going to tie my hands and ankles?' asked Noella, quickly settling herself on the bed.

Edmund smiled, and there was something about the smile that disturbed her. 'No, I don't think so. You see, this is going to be a test of your self-control. I want you to be free to move, but I also want you to keep still. Do you understand?'

'No,' said Noella, who wasn't in the mood for self-control after hearing Harriet's sounds of total abandonment.

'I'm going to do all the things you like in order to bring you to a climax,' said Edmund patiently, as though speaking to a child. 'The only thing is that if you move in any way, even inadvertently, then I go back to the beginning and start again. How long it takes will all depend on you. I think that should be fun, do you agree?'

Noella shook her head. 'I don't want games, Edmund. Can't we just make love quickly? I want to feel you inside me. I'm ready now, I don't need all these preliminaries.'

Edmund's forehead creased in a slight frown. 'I do hope you're not in danger of becoming boring, Noella. You know very well that I prefer an inventive love life.'

'Yes, but . . .'

He sighed. 'All right, let's forget it and go to sleep. It's been a long day and—'

'No!' exclaimed Noella sharply. 'I want you to make love to me.'

'And I want to make love to you,' he assured her. 'If it proves as interesting as I anticipate then perhaps we could play it with Harriet some time. She sounds as though she might benefit from some discipline before she's allowed satisfaction.'

Noella smiled. 'That's true.' Resigned now to a long evening she waited for Edmund to begin.

He stared down at her, at the lush curves of her wonderfully feminine body, and his erection began to hurt him it was so hard. Picking up a tube of lubricating jelly he put some on his fingers and then began to spread it around Noella's nipples and the surrounding area.

The jelly was cool and sweetly scented. Within seconds Noella could feel the edge of the leather suit cutting into the soft undersides of her breasts as they began to swell. Edmund's hands massaged more firmly and she sighed with pleasure, arching her back slightly to increase the pressure. At once Edmund's hands stopped moving, and then they were removed altogether leaving Noella without any stimulation. 'You moved,' he said softly.

'Hardly at all,' she exclaimed in surprise. 'Surely that doesn't count?'

'It all counts,' he whispered. 'Now, I'll begin again.'

Once more he massaged the jelly on to her breasts, and this time Noella concentrated all her attention on keeping still, trying to blot out the sensations of pleasure that were flowing through her nerve endings.

'Good girl,' he murmured and next she felt him drawing down the zip at the front of the costume so that he could slip his hand inside the tight-fitting leather and knead her sensitive abdominal muscles.

For several minutes she managed to lie there completely still, simply revelling in the sensations, but then the pressure eased a little and without thinking she pushed up against his hand. To her horror he promptly zipped the suit up again and once more her body was left untouched.

'You were doing really well,' he said in apparent regret.

'I can't play this game!' shouted Noella, now almost angry with mounting frustration. 'It's not possible to keep still.'

'Then we'll sleep,' he said coolly.

But Noella's body was far too aroused for sleep and they both knew it. She gave a groan of despair which he knew was assent and then his hands were on her breasts once more.

This time Noella did really well. Edmund was

even able to finish massaging her stomach without her moving and then he turned his attention to the space between her spread legs, the very core of Noella's sexuality where she felt herself to be on fire with waiting.

'How damp you are,' he whispered as he stroked her gently with one finger along her outer sex lips.

Noella felt an overwhelming desire to squirm against the soft fleece of the sheepskin beneath her but managed to control herself. As Edmund's finger pressed down and her outer sex lips parted, she nearly moved her right leg to assist him but again remembered just in time that it was forbidden.

Smiling to himself, Edmund continued to press down with his finger until he located the tiny swollen bud of her clitoris. He then maintained a soft steady pressure that resulted in a gradual build-up of sexual tension behind Noella's pubic bone, a tension that finally could go no further without some different movement from Edmund.

Edmund, however, had no intention of providing that movement. Instead, keeping his finger where it was, he lay down beside his spread-eagled wife and with his free hand drew a ribbon of silk across each of her breasts in turn.

Noella was almost demented by excitement and frustration. She longed for some kind of movement between her thighs, some change of tempo that would enable her body to continue surging towards its orgasm, but she didn't dare move in case Edmund decided to start the whole process over again. There were tiny drops of perspiration on her upper lip and Edmund licked them away tenderly, allowing his tongue to slip between her teeth for a moment in an imitation of the thrusting movement that he knew she wanted to feel between her legs.

All at once a nerve jumped in Noella's right leg and she felt it twitch. She looked at Edmund with something close to despair. 'It's not my fault, it's like cramp,' she assured him, straining to keep the rest of her still.

Edmund nodded, and then at last he allowed his finger to move around her clitoris, massaging the whole area with firm rotations until the resulting sensations caused Noella's eyes to widen as she struggled to remain still.

'You're doing very well,' Edmund told her, 'I expect you'd like the little black twins now, wouldn't you?'

Noella shook her head. Normally she loved the tiny bullet-shaped black probes that Edmund would insert within her front and back passages at the same time, before turning on the power so that the pulsations would vibrate through her from front to back, causing her some of her most fulfilling climaxes, but not under these conditions, not when she wasn't allowed to move her legs and buck with ecstasy.

'I'd rather not,' she gasped.

Again Edmund gave her one of his less than reassuring smiles. 'But you like them. I remember last time we used them you kept having one climax after another.'

'I won't be able to keep still!' she gasped.

'Of course you will,' said Edmund smoothly. 'After all the games we've played over the years I expected you to be more adventurous than this, you know.'

Noella bit on her lower lip and finally nodded agreement. His fingers had already opened her up and her muscles there were tight as she held them rigid to guard against unintentional movement.

'I knew you'd agree,' he said with satisfaction, and within seconds she felt the lubricated tip of one probe being eased into her rectum as Edmund let the other play softly over the moist tissue around her clitoris. They were vibrating on a low setting but after all that had gone before, Noella knew that she would come in a very short time, and she prayed that her body wouldn't betray her during these last few moments.

Edmund watched her struggling to keep still and admired her self-control. He was also incredibly excited by the sight of her subduing her normal sexual exuberance, and when her leg muscles rippled with tension he wanted to take her immediately, but instead turned up the speed on the twin vibrators and watched as her orgasm rushed nearer.

For Noella this was always the best moment of all. The moment when every nerve ending was at its most sensitive, when her senses were so finely tuned that it felt as though she'd shed her skin. She began to utter tiny sounds deep in her throat. Her breasts were larger than Edmund had ever seen them, and just as all the glorious sensations were drawing together before erupting into release he couldn't resist tugging on her right nipple, drawing it out as far as possible and then tweaking it between his finger and thumb.

With a cry, Noella's whole body jerked and her hips lifted off the bed as the highly stimulated nerve endings sent messages of impending ecstasy to her brain. The movement was involuntary and the moment she'd made it Noella shouted aloud in despair and then tried to push herself over the edge into release before Edmund could stop her, but he was too quick. With one swift movement he removed the twin probes and released her breast leaving her stranded on the very brink of what she knew would have been an incredible climax.

'What a pity,' he said softly. 'Now we have to begin all over again.'

Noella's screams of fury at being left frustrated could be heard in the next room and Harriet stirred in Lewis's arms.

'What on earth's going on in there?' she asked sleepily.

'I've no idea,' said Lewis. 'Probably another of their arguments.'

'It didn't sound like an argument a few moments ago,' laughed Harriet.

'Well perhaps he disappointed her.'

'I doubt it,' said Harriet thoughtfully.

'You mean he looks like a man who'd know how to please?' queried Lewis, his voice amused.

Harriet snuggled closer to him, her breasts brushing against his chest. 'I suppose so, yes.'

'He does want you. You know that, don't you?'

'Yes,' admitted Harriet.

'And you'd love to know what he's like in bed, isn't that true?' he persisted.

Harriet sighed. 'Lewis, we've only just got married. I don't need anyone but you. I love you and I don't want to lose you.'

'We're not talking above love,' Lewis reminded her. 'We're talking about desire. Now, isn't it true that you desire Edmund?'

'No.'

Lewis laughed and hugged her tighter. 'You're a fibber. You desire him but you don't want to do anything about it because you don't think that you should. There's nothing wrong with desire, it's perfectly normal.'

'Not when you've just got married!' exclaimed Harriet.

'We've been lovers for over two years now. Hasn't "*custom staled our infinite variety*" as the Bard once said?'

'All right,' she conceded. 'I suppose I would like to know what he was like. He's very attractive, in an unusual kind of way.'

'What's unusual about him?' asked Lewis with an air of detached interest that Harriet found rather disturbing. 'I'd have said he was a typical product of the English public school system, except for the fact that he prefers women to men.'

'I suppose it's the fact that he seems on the surface to be exactly what you say. He's very smooth and urbane, and at first there's no obvious sexual magnetism about him, but as soon as you start talking to him and really look into his eyes, you get this feeling that he isn't what he's pretending to be. There's something almost dangerous about him. When Noella said earlier that he'd "gone on the turn" I wasn't surprised because that's the feeling he gives me, that he could turn, and probably into something much more exciting than the conventional image he chooses to present to the world.'

'You've certainly given him some thought,' laughed Lewis.

'Only because you've encouraged me.'

Lewis's arms tightened round her. 'Oh no, Harriet. I think we should both be quite honest about this. I saw the way you looked at him on the day of our wedding, and it wasn't the way you look at most people. Even then, long before I'd told you about this film, you were interested.'

'I might have been,' conceded Harriet reluctantly, 'but I wouldn't have done anything about it if—'

'You haven't done anything about it now, and you don't have to if that's not what you want,' interrupted Lewis. 'I can't stop Edmund lusting after you, but the rest is entirely up to you. Whatever happens, Harriet, you're not coming back to me when it's over and saying I *made* you do anything, because that's not the way things happen. You're an adult and you make your own decisions. Do what you want, but at least have the decency to take the responsibility yourself.'

'That's not fair!' exclaimed Harriet. 'If you'd only tell me that you don't want me to respond to Edmund, that I'm your wife now and you expect fidelity, then I'd never think of going with him, however strong my desire.'

'I'm your husband, not your gaoler. I don't suppose for one moment that I'll remain faithful to you for the rest of our lives, so how can I possibly demand the same thing of you?' he asked casually.

Harriet felt as though he'd slapped her. 'You mean you'll have affairs?'

'Let's not be naïve about this. I had an affair with you while I was married to Rowena, why should I have changed? I'm not saying I'd fall in love with another woman, in fact that's most unlikely, but sexual fidelity isn't high on my list of priorities.'

'Then why did you want us to get married?' asked a bewildered Harriet.

'Because I'm in love with you.'

'But if you're in love with me how can you—'

'Harriet, you are being incredibly unsophisticated and it doesn't suit you,' said Lewis, his voice beginning to take on a hard edge. 'If you wanted a conventional marriage and an ordinary life then you should have married that merchant banker you were running away from when we first met. This is a different world, darling, and if you're the woman I think you are, you'll enjoy it to the full.'

In the silence that followed his remark they both heard a cry of ecstatic pleasure from Noella, followed a few seconds later by another and then a third. Harriet shivered. The cries were almost too intense, as though the pleasure had gone far beyond anything Harriet had ever experienced.

'Sounds as though they've kissed and made up,' murmured Lewis laconically.

'I don't want to lose you,' said Harriet huskily.

'You won't lose me, unless you ask me to go,' he assured her.

'But suppose I find that Edmund's addictive?'

'I'm afraid,' said Lewis slowly, 'that's a risk we both have to take.'

'Why?'

'Because if we don't there won't be a film.'

Harriet was suddenly filled with rage. 'Do your films mean more to you than I do?' she demanded.

'I think we'd better go to sleep now,' said Lewis softly. 'There are some questions, Harriet, that are better left unanswered.'

Chapter Three

THE NEXT MORNING when Harriet awoke the sun was streaming through their windows. Slipping out of bed, she opened the curtains slightly and saw that it was a perfect summer's morning. A few fluffy white clouds moved lazily across the blue sky and there was a soft dew on the grass. From the window she could see the figure of a man – Oliver Kesby she assumed – cleaning the surface of the outdoor pool with a large net; the water looked clear and inviting.

'The rain's stopped, Lewis,' she said happily.

Lewis mumbled something unintelligible and rolled onto his back, shielding his eyes from the light. 'What time is it?'

'Half-past eight. Why don't we go for a walk before breakfast? We could explore the grounds.'

'You go,' he said sleepily. 'My legs won't function until I've had coffee, especially not when I'm jet lagged.'

'I think I heard Mrs Webster tap on the door, she might have left an early morning tray outside,' said Harriet, crossing the room to open it. She was entirely naked and Lewis felt himself hardening at the sight of her long slim body with its softly rounded breasts and deliciously small waist. Once again he was struck by the realisation of exactly what he was risking by going ahead with his film, but he had to know the truth of where people's desires could lead them even when they were at their happiest. He wanted to know not only for his film but also for himself. Until he did he would never feel secure with Harriet.

Unaware of her husband's own fears, Harriet had resolved during the night that she would do exactly what he said and follow her desires. If Edmund continued to prove attractive to her and an affair became possible, then she'd have one. She had a suspicion that deep down she was no different from Lewis. Certainly an unconventional life made her feel more alive if not as safe as the one she'd envisaged when she was a young girl.

'Sorry,' she exclaimed as she placed the tray on the bedside table. 'Mrs Webster's only left us tea. You'll have to get used to it while we're in England.'

'I'll never get used to it,' muttered Lewis grumpily.

Harriet ignored him. She drank a cup herself, pulled a hyacinth-coloured sundress on over a short sleeved white T-shirt, thrust her feet into a pair of white canvas shoes and then hurried out of the house. Once outside she took several deep breaths and felt her whole body relaxing. Everywhere seemed totally peaceful. Birds were singing in the distance and somewhere far off some children were playing, but here at Penruan all was silent.

Oliver Kesby watched Harriet coming across the lawn towards the pool and decided that she was far more beautiful than the woman he'd met the previous night. Although she lacked that woman's sophistication, she had an air of free sexuality about her that set his imagination racing.

He'd heard of Lewis James and had enjoyed *Dark Secret* more than anything he'd ever seen, but somehow this girl – for that was all she looked in her simple T-shirt and sundress – didn't fit with his image of the kind of woman such a man would choose for his wife. The blonde would have fitted the bill better he thought as he smiled at the approaching young woman.

Harriet smiled back at him. She could quite see why Noella had found him attractive, although he wasn't Harriet's type. His well-built muscular body, obviously kept in trim by weight-lifting, rippled beneath a tight blue T-shirt, and his legs, clad only in brief shorts, were tanned and well muscled. When he smiled, his light blue eyes glinted in the framework of their surprisingly dark lashes.

'It's a lovely morning,' she exclaimed.

'We've had a good couple of weeks,' he assured her. 'Yesterday was an exception.'

Harriet crouched down and trailed a hand in the water of the pool. It was cool, but not unbearably cold. 'Is it going to stay nice?' she asked.

'So they say, at least for the next week. Where are your friends?' he said.

'Still asleep. I think they are all feeling jet lagged, but I'm too excited to stay in bed.'

'Excited?'

'At being back here. I've got so many happy memories of the place. We always spent our holidays here when I was a child, and I was longing to see it again. We're on our honeymoon,' she added proudly.

Oliver nodded. 'I'd heard that, well, read it in the papers to be more accurate. You're not American then?'

'Of course not; I'm very, very English. Will the pool be warm enough to swim in later on?'

'Depends on what you're used to. It's never like an indoor pool, but the sun should warm it up nicely.'

'Then I'll swim this afternoon.' Straightening up she caught his eyes on her and recognised the look only too well. 'Do you and your family live close by?' she asked.

'I live in a cottage on the grounds; my wife left me a couple of years ago. I have no family here. My only relations live in Surrey, and I don't have anything to do with them any more.'

Harriet didn't like to ask why. For a few minutes she and Oliver made more small talk, but then she turned away, anxious to be alone for a time.

'Will your friends be using the pool too?' Oliver called after her.

'Probably,' replied Harriet, who had no doubt that provided Oliver stayed in the vicinity Noella would be only too happy to put on a costume and at least make a pretence of swimming in the pool.

'Sometimes it's a mistake to try and go back,' he added, and hearing his words Harriet shivered, despite the warmth of the sun.

Oliver returned to removing leaves from the water. He'd read Harriet very well. She wasn't interested in him, and she never would be. Well, that wasn't a problem, he couldn't really blame her. With Lewis James for a husband, and a brand new husband at that, he wasn't likely to have much to offer. On the other hand, her friend Noella had already made her interest clear and since he was without a girlfriend at the moment he thought that if anything developed there he might, just this once, break his rule about mixing with the summer visitors.

By the time Harriet got back indoors Lewis and Noella were both up and dressed, although there was no sign of Edmund. 'You're an early bird,' said Noella, who was wearing tight-fitting white jeans and a multi-coloured silk shirt with short sleeves.

'It's the best time of the day,' retorted Harriet. 'I

saw your hunk as well. He was busy cleaning the pool.'

'Don't you agree he's gorgeous?' asked Noella with a laugh.

'He certainly looks good in shorts and a T-shirt; the only trouble is, I think he knows it. Besides, I never trust men who work out a lot.'

'How do you know he works out a lot?' enquired Lewis, drinking his third cup of coffee.

'You can always tell. No one has bulging arm muscles just by eating their greens. Anyway, he says the pool will be warm enough to use this afternoon, so I thought we might give it a try.'

'As long as he cleans it while I use it then I'm game,' agreed Noella. 'Here, there's a letter for you, honey. I found it on the mat when I was checking the mail for Edmund.'

Harriet frowned. 'But no one knows I'm here.'

'Someone must,' Lewis pointed out. 'What's the postmark?'

Harriet studied it. 'London, and I seem to recognise the handwriting.' She slit open the envelope and drew out the letter. 'It's from Ella,' she said with pleasure. 'I forgot, I told her we'd be here when I wrote to her about the wedding. You remember me telling you about Ella, Lewis?'

'Your actress friend? Sure, I remember.'

Harriet's eyes scanned the four pages of looped writing. 'Ella's suffering from a broken heart,' she said when she'd finished reading. 'Simon's left her for an older woman and she's devastated. She's also out of work and broke.'

'A happy letter,' laughed Lewis.

'Well, she makes light of it all and sends her love to us both, but I can tell that she's pretty upset. Lewis, why don't we invite her to stay here for a couple of weeks? The house is large enough, and if it weren't for Ella, you and I would never have met. She's the one who persuaded me to answer your advert when you were staying in London.'

Lewis frowned. 'But she'd only feel out of it, Harriet. There's nothing worse than being on your own and surrounded by couples.'

'She won't be surrounded by couples, there are only four of us in all.'

'Just the same it might make her feel worse.'

Harriet sat down next to him and put a hand on his arm. 'Don't you think she might add a little something to your plot?' she whispered teasingly.

Lewis raised his eyebrows. 'You think it needs more complications?'

'I think it might benefit from a larger cast.'

'Harriet, think carefully about this. Do you really want Ella to join us? Is she the kind of girl who'd fit in with everyone else?'

'Ella gets on with anyone,' Harriet assured him.

He glanced across the room to where Noella was leafing through a brochure on Cornwall. 'And exactly where will Ella fit into my film?' he enquired.

'I've no idea,' admitted Harriet. 'But as she's a very pretty, lively girl, and an actress as well, perhaps you'll discover a forbidden desire of your own.'

'She's forbidden is she?' he asked, a smile playing round his mouth.

'She's my best friend!' exclaimed Harriet. 'I've shared a lot with her, but I think I draw the line at my husband.'

'Well, that's certainly interesting, and will doubtless add to her appeal even more,' remarked Lewis. 'Okay then, if you're sure it's what you want, go ahead and invite her here. Noella and I had decided we'd have a trip into Polperro this morning, as soon as Edmund manages to get himself out of bed.'

'Fine,' said Harriet, but she was too distracted by his words about Ella to be very interested in their plans. For a long time she sat with Ella's letter in her hands and thought about what could happen if Lewis really were to fall for her friend, but in the end she decided she was being ridiculous and scrawled a hasty invitation. After all, she reasoned to herself, Lewis would have his hands full with his film. An additional distraction would surely be more than he could handle.

Finally Edmund emerged from his bedroom and, finding Harriet alone in the large kitchen, sat down next to her. 'Where are the other two?'

'Noella's having a look at the pool and Lewis is on the phone to Mark.'

'You mean Mark's here already?'

Harriet nodded. 'Lewis finds it hard to survive without a scriptwriter close to hand.'

'I can't imagine why he needs him on his honeymoon,' remarked Edmund. 'I suppose they're working on the sequel to *Dark Secret*, is that it?'

'Yes.'

'Interesting. What's it about, do you know?'

'I don't think Lewis is too sure yet,' said Harriet with perfect honesty.

'Has it got a working title?' persisted Edmund.

Harriet felt uneasy. His eyes were sharp with intelligence and she had the distinct feeling he might have a suspicion about what was happening. 'You'll have to ask him yourself,' she said quickly. 'I won't talk film business on my honeymoon.'

'If you were married to me, I wouldn't expect you to,' Edmund assured her. 'Believe me, Harriet, I can think of far more interesting things we could do.'

Harriet smiled. 'I'm sure you can.'

'Do you ever imagine things like that?' he murmured.

'Like what?'

'Like what we could do together.'

Harriet lowered her eyes, but he could see a pulse beating in the hollow at the base of her neck. 'No,' she said softly.

Edmund stood up, resting a hand gently on her shoulder. 'I'm not altogether sure I believe that,' he said casually.

'You obviously have a doubting nature.'

'Not at all, but I think I know quite a lot about women.'

'So does Lewis,' Harriet assured him.

Edmund smiled. 'I know that, the walls here might be thick, but it's still possible to hear things in the silence of the night.'

Harriet stared up at him, her grey eyes frank. 'I know – we heard Noella.'

'Indeed? And what kind of noise did Noella make?'

Harriet hesitated. 'I thought at first it was – you know – one of pleasure, later I wasn't quite so sure.'

'Then you're a very clever young woman,' he said smoothly.

Half-fascinated and half-disturbed, Harriet watched him leave the room, and once again she wondered about the sounds she'd heard from their bedroom and their real significance.

Later, Lewis drove them all to Polperro, leaving the car parked at the top of a steep hill on the edge of the village. 'We'll walk down,' he said to a horrified Noella. 'It's useless trying to park any nearer, and anyway the views are incredible.'

Hand in hand, he and Harriet led the way, while Noella and Edmund followed behind them, Noella clutching Edmund's arm as she struggled not to turn her ankles in her high-heeled sandals.

Looking up at the houses set on the sides of the sharply rising hills surrounding the village, Harriet could recall in minute detail the childish excitement of her earlier visits. 'There used to be a wonderful fudge shop half-way along the main street,' she told the others. 'We must make sure we get some while we're here.'

'If we don't I think I'll leave it. I'm sure as hell never doing this again,' gasped Noella, as strands of her blonde hair escaped from her french pleat.

'I rather think you're a child of the city,' remarked Edmund mildly. 'Don't worry, we won't have to climb all the way back up. They run a pony and trap for people like you, I read it in the guide book.'

'Do you ride, Harriet?' asked Noella, when they were in the main street and the slope was less steep.

'Not really.'

'You should, it's very sexy. I've had some of my best orgasms on horseback.'

A passing tourist looked at her in astonishment and Harriet couldn't help laughing. 'That doesn't say very much for me,' said Edmund mildly. 'I knew you were into whips, but I didn't realise you needed the horse as well.'

Harriet's mouth went dry at the images her mind was conjuring up. 'You're not shocked are you?' asked Noella, seeing the younger woman's expression. 'Don't you and Lewis enjoy a little mild S&M?'

'We don't like anything wild,' said Lewis, kissing Harriet on the side of her neck.

Harriet was grateful for the intimacy of the gesture and turned her face to his so that he could kiss her on the mouth as they continued walking along.

'Now there I rather agree with you,' commented Edmund. 'It's Noella who draws the

61

boundary lines. Left to myself I'd probably be far more extreme.'

'He's kidding,' Noella confided. 'He isn't nearly as wild as he's making out.'

'It's difficult to imagine,' said Harriet. 'Even in casual clothes he always looks so conventional.'

'Well, looks can be misleading. I definitely wouldn't say he was conventional, it's just that he likes to experiment, but then don't all men?'

'I suppose so,' conceded Harriet.

'You know, I've had a lot of lovers,' continued Noella, not troubling to drop her voice at all. 'And I mean a lot, but I've never met anyone like Edmund, and I'd sure as hell hate to lose him.'

'Why should you lose him?' asked Harriet as the two men walked over to look at the Pilchard Inn, where fishermen had once gone to have their fish weighed.

Noella looked thoughtfully at her. 'I'm not sure. There was a time, not that long ago, when I felt quite secure. After all, I'm his third wife, Edmund's money isn't limitless, and sexually we're very well matched but recently I've begun to get the impression that he's tiring of me.'

'Perhaps he's just tired,' suggested Harriet. 'Lewis says Edmund works very hard without seeming to work at all. The holiday might be exactly what he needs.'

'I think it might,' agreed Noella. 'The trouble is, I'm not sure that his needs and mine are quite the same.'

'Meaning what?'

'Come on, Harriet,' exclaimed Noella, 'let's not kid each other. My husband's very taken with you and he isn't bothering to hide it from either of us.'

'I'm on my honeymoon,' laughed Harriet.

'Yeah, well stranger things have happened. I remember that as soon as I was married to my first husband, I started fancying every male in sight. Some kind of reaction against being tied down I guess.'

'I don't feel tied down,' protested Harriet.

'Maybe not, but you fancy Edmund.'

'And if I do,' said Harriet evenly, 'will that be the first time you've ever met another woman who fancied him?'

'Of course not.'

'Then why are you worried?'

'Because there's something that makes me think you might be two of a kind. I don't care a fig about his affairs, I've had plenty of my own, but I don't fancy being another ex-Mrs Mitchell.'

'What about Lewis?' asked Harriet. 'Can you put your hand on your heart and say that you don't fancy my husband too?'

Noella shook her head. 'It's not the same, sweetie. Every woman who meets Lewis fancies him, but that doesn't mean he's going to fancy them. Lewis would never be interested in me, I'm not his type, but I know that Edmund fancies you.'

'Is this a warning of some kind?' asked Harriet, lowering her voice as the men started to walk back towards them.

'Hell no, I've never tried to warn anyone off

63

Edmund, that would only add to the attraction. I'm just telling you I know what's happening.'

'Nothing's happening,' retorted Harriet.

'Not yet, but it will,' said Noella, and then she smiled brightly at her husband. 'Come on, Edmund. I want to take a look at one of these famous views Lewis has been telling us about. How can we get up these cliffs and take a look for ourselves?'

'There's a cliff path by the harbour,' said Harriet, taking hold of Lewis's hand again. 'If you've got the energy you can go up the steps there and then round the back of some cottages where the path opens out a bit. There are one or two seats and the most incredible views imaginable.'

'I've got the energy,' said Noella firmly.

Harriet and Lewis decided to stay and look at the small fishing boats in the harbour while the other two set off up the cliff path. Once they were alone Lewis pulled Harriet against him, kissing her gently on the mouth and letting his tongue slide round her teeth and along her gums until she started to squirm.

'Happy?' he asked when he released her.

'Very happy.'

'What was Noella talking to you about?'

'Nothing much; she seems to think that Edmund's tiring of her, but I'm sure she's being paranoid.'

'I'm sure she's not. Noella's far too sensible to worry unless she's got something to worry about.

Besides, ten years is the longest Edmund's ever remained married to one woman. He's always searching for the perfect companion, a soul mate as well as a sexual partner. Probably my good luck has made him restless.'

'You don't really want me to sleep with him, do you?' whispered Harriet.

'I want you to do whatever you want to do,' repeated Lewis, giving her another kiss before glancing up at the sky. 'It's clouding over a bit. I think we ought to get back to Penruan, especially if you girls are hoping to swim after lunch.'

'Aren't we having lunch here?'

Lewis shook his head. 'I want to make love to you before we eat. That might prove a little difficult in the middle of Polperro.'

'I'll go up and fetch the other two,' said Harriet quickly, already anticipating the delights that lay ahead of her. She hurried up the stone steps and then looked around. The whole area was deserted, all the seats were empty and Noella and Edmund seemed to have vanished.

Harriet walked towards the edge of the cliff top and then, just round the curve of the bend, she saw Noella and Edmund on the grass between the rocks. Noella was crouched down looking out to sea and Edmund was sitting right behind her, his body touching hers, with his arms tightly round her waist and his legs spread out in front of him. At first Harriet thought they were simply looking out to sea, but then she saw Noella's body rise and fall slightly, and a flash of pink skin at the top of her legs showed that her jeans must be round her ankles. With her heart beating loudly in her ears Harriet continued to watch as Noella moved more and more rapidly, and Edmund's hands assisted her as she slid up and down on his erection.

Harriet knew that she shouldn't continue to watch, but she couldn't make herself move. She was terrified that someone else would come up the steps and realise what was happening, and at the same time filled with admiration at what they were doing. As Noella approached her climax and uttered a moan of excitement a seagull, alarmed by the noise, flew off a nearby rock and across the sea, but Harriet remained where she was and when Noella's head was thrown back and Edmund's hands had to tighten to keep her in place, Harriet could almost feel the warmth of the other woman's orgasm sweeping over her and she felt herself growing damp between her thighs.

She waited for Edmund to finish, but once Noella's body had slumped into a position of satisfied relaxation, he lifted her off him and as she pulled up her jeans, he stood up and his hand moved to fasten his flies. It seemed that he was content to wait until later for his own satisfaction.

Quickly Harriet turned to go, but she was too late because at the same moment, Edmund turned and caught her standing there, her cheeks flushed and her lips slightly parted with the excitement of what she'd seen. 'Come to look at the view?' he asked sardonically.

'I've only just got here,' said Harriet quickly. 'Lewis says that we'd better be getting back. He doesn't want to eat here, he'd rather go back to Penruan.'

'Why?' asked Noella, facing Harriet with a triumphant smile on her face.

'I think he wants a rest before lunch.'

'You mean a lie down rather than a rest I take it?' suggested Edmund.

'At least we're on our honeymoon,' responded Harriet.

'You mean sex before lunch is reserved for honeymooners?'

Harriet was flustered. 'No, of course not. I just meant – oh, forget it. Are you coming or not?'

'It appears not. I can't say the same for Noella, however. Don't look so cross,' he added with a smile. 'We'll be with you in a minute or two.'

They took the pony and trap back up the hill to the end of the village, and then walked the last hundred yards to the car park. Noella chatted all the time, saying how beautiful the village was and how amazed she'd been by the view, but Harriet was quiet and during the drive back Lewis asked her if she was all right.

'I'm fine,' she said, trying to erase the image of Noella moving up and down on Edmund's lap while the waves crashed onto the rocks below them.

'Not tired? I wondered if the jet lag was catching up with you.'

'No,' she said quickly, 'I'm not tired.'

He put out a hand and squeezed her knee. 'That's good.'

Back at Penruan, Noella disappeared to have a rest, Edmund went into the lounge to make some telephone calls. Lewis started to go up the stairs towards their bedroom but Harriet stopped him.

'Let's do it somewhere else,' she said huskily.

'Sure, where did you have in mind?'

'Outside somewhere, in the grounds?'

He shook his head. 'I don't think we can. I saw Oliver wandering around when we got back.'

'There must be somewhere,' said Harriet, still unable to get the picture of Edmund and Noella out of her mind.

'I know. How about the conservatory? It should be warm enough with the sun on it, and the furniture there looks comfortable. There's always the risk that someone might see through the french windows, but—'

'I don't care about the risk,' said Harriet. 'Please, Lewis, let's try the conservatory.'

'Anything to keep my wife happy!' he agreed cheerfully.

The conservatory was large and warm, the glass roof making it exceptionally light as well. A thickly padded two-seater wicker sofa seemed the most comfortable place and Lewis was just about to take off his clothes when Harriet stopped him. 'Keep them on,' she murmured. 'I want you inside me now. I don't want to wait any longer.'

Lewis looked thoughtfully at her. 'What were Edmund and Noella up to on the cliff top?'

'Nothing, well, they were looking at the view but nothing else, why?'

'Because you haven't seemed the same since you went to fetch them. I'd rather undress, Harriet. I like to feel your skin against mine.'

Harriet hesitated, but then quickly started to take off her sundress, peeling off the T-shirt beneath with almost indecent haste so that Lewis could see that she hadn't bothered with any underwear that morning.

As soon as he was naked he went to lie Harriet down on the sofa but this time she was determined to have things her own way. 'Sit on the edge,' she said, almost frantic for them to get on with it. 'Then I can sit on top of you.'

He obeyed, but instead of sitting on his lap facing him, as she usually did, Harriet stood with her back to him, put her legs on each side of his and then eased herself onto his rock-hard erection, feeling the satisfying width of him as it filled her aching emptiness.

Lewis ran his hands up over her ribs until they cupped the undersides of her breasts, feeling the softly swelling flesh in his palms. He kissed the side of her neck and his fingers began to tease her rigid nipples.

'No, grip my waist, please,' she urged him.

'I'm enjoying this,' protested Lewis, still half-amused by her apparent inability to wait.

'I want you to hold my waist,' she said fiercely, and for the first time Lewis began to have a suspicion about what was happening. Even so he complied, but inside he felt a moment's disquiet.

As his hands gripped each side of her body Harriet started to rise and fall in small movements, as similar to Noella's as she could manage. 'Help me!' she gasped, and taking up her rhythm Lewis began to raise and lower her until the smouldering heat, that had lingered between her thighs ever since the moment she'd seen Noella and Edmund on the clifftop, started to flare outwards and her belly tightened with an impending climax.

'Slow down,' whispered Lewis. 'If you're not careful it will all be over too soon.'

'I want it to be over,' cried Harriet. 'I need to come now,' and she tried to increase the pace.

Lewis could tell by her breathing and the soft receptive moistness of her internal walls gripping his erection that she was almost ready to climax, but he could also tell that this had nothing to do with him. She'd been aroused and wanting sex from the moment she'd returned to him at Polperro harbour.

Now his hands were less than gentle around her waist and he moved her so rapidly that even she was taken by surprise. The tendrils of arousal turned into stabbing spears that lanced through her entire body and then every muscle in her started to go rigid as her climax approached.

Lewis was determined not to be left behind and he let all thoughts of a long drawn-out session of lovemaking fade away as he too was caught up in her frantic urgency. As the walls of her vagina began to tighten around him in the first spasms of her orgasm, he felt the highly sensitive tip of his penis tingle even more intensely. Harriet reached behind her and drew her fingernails lightly over his hipbone; he gasped and then his orgasm rushed upwards at the same time as Harriet's body finally went into an almost painfully intense series of muscular contractions that left her shattered and totally replete.

Outside the french windows, Oliver Kesby watched in silence, his manhood pressing painfully against the constrictions of his shorts. He resolved there and then that this time he was definitely going to get involved with his new tenants.

'That was incredible,' breathed Harriet, falling back against Lewis.

Lewis didn't reply, and neither did he pull her closer and cuddle her as he normally did after lovemaking. Instead he put her none too gently to one side and started to pick up his clothes. 'The next time Edmund and Noella turn you on, I suggest you use them to satisfy you as well,' he said shortly. 'I like to know I have your full attention at times like this.'

Harriet looked at him in dismay. 'Didn't you enjoy it?'

'It was good sex if that's what you mean. Unfortunately I had something more intimate in mind.'

'You're the one who wants me to be turned on by Edmund!' shouted Harriet as he walked out of the conservatory. 'What's the matter, don't you like your own storyline?'

As he made his way upstairs, Lewis was asking himself the same thing.

Chapter Four

By mid-afternoon even Noella agreed that it was warm enough to use the outdoor pool, and, armed with sunscreen, a floppy scarlet straw hat and a knee-length cotton cover-up, she set out across the lawns. Harriet, who simply took a T-shirt to slip over her bikini, wondered why it was that the Americans made every pleasure, from enjoying the sun to eating clotted cream, seem like a sin.

Edmund had a pair of hand-made Italian slacks on over his swimming trunks but his chest was bare and Harriet couldn't help comparing his body with that of Lewis. Where Lewis's chest was covered in a profusion of dark hair, Edmund's lightly tanned skin only had small amounts of curly brown hair around his nipples that travelled down in a thin line that disected his stomach and thickened slightly before it disappeared beneath the waistband of his slacks. He was of slighter build than Lewis, but not as slender as Harriet had expected and his tight chest muscles suggested that he kept himself very fit.

'Where's Lewis?' asked Edmund, walking beside Harriet while Noella went on ahead.

'On the telephone, as usual. He said he'll join us in a few minutes.'

'Is the bikini for swimming in, or purely decorative purposes?' he enquired with a smile.

'Oh it's multi-functional. I can look decorative and swim at the same time.'

'I'm sure you can; in fact, it's hard to imagine you looking anything other than decorative,' he observed.

'Hey, these loungers are quite comfortable,' called Noella, settling herself down beside the pool and covering herself liberally with sun cream.

'For someone who's so bothered about the sun you've got a very good tan,' remarked Harriet.

'Fake, honey. It's all from a bottle; you won't catch me burning in the sun or frying to death on a sunbed. Edmund, can you do my back for me?'

Edmund took the bottle from her and then spread the lotion over her shoulders, legs and arms, all of which were left exposed by her striking blue and white swimsuit with its contrasting diagonal floral pattern. 'Roll over, I'll do your back,' he said when he'd finished, and with a sigh of contentment Noella obeyed.

Watching him work the lotion into Noella's skin, Harriet tried to imagine how his supple fingers would feel on her flesh, and what the sensation would be like if the fingers were then to stray into the inside of her bikini bottom.

'Keep right on, sweetheart,' whispered Noella when he'd finished but Edmund merely straightened up and turned to Harriet.

'Would you like some on you? We don't want you getting burnt and having to stay out of the sun for the next week.'

Harriet stared at him, her eyes wide; he stared back at her, his fingers gripping the tube of suncream tightly. 'Perhaps that's a good idea,' she conceded, 'although I don't usually burn.'

'Lie down on the lounger next to Noella's. I'll start with your back.' His voice was brisk and impersonal, and Harriet wondered if she'd imagined the look of desire in his eyes a moment earlier. Stretching out on her stomach she tensed in anticipation of his first touch.

'Relax,' he said softly. 'What do you think I'm going to do to you?'

'I hate the first bit of cream going on, it's always so cold,' said Harriet, hoping he'd accept her explanation.

'Personally I like contrasts,' he responded, his fingers moving lazily over her flesh. 'Cold cream on hot skin, warm water on cold flesh, they're exquisite contrasts.'

His fingers were exquisite too. They skimmed across the surface of her body and brought every nerve ending to life so that when he'd finished she tingled all over her back. 'Now for the front,' he said calmly. Harriet rolled over, keeping her eyes closed to blot out the sight of him. As his fingers touched the fragile bones at the base of her neck she felt a sudden surge of desire and her nipples hardened, brushing against the flimsy fabric of her bikini. Her stomach muscles jumped nervously and she deliberately tried to slow her breathing as a wonderful glowing sensation began to spread through her.

With careful strokes of his fingers, Edmund spread the cream across the exposed tops of her breasts, now thrust upwards by her position, and he felt the tissue swell beneath his hands. Without thinking, Harriet gave a soft sigh and arched her back a little to allow him easier access.

'What's going on here?' called Lewis, his voice breaking into her sensual reverie.

'Harriet was worried she'd burn,' explained Edmund, offering the tube to Lewis. 'Here, you take over.'

Harriet opened her eyes and stared up at the two men standing over her. Lewis looked down at her, his dark eyes unfathomable. 'You carry on,' he said to Edmund, after only the slightest hesitation. 'I've got some more calls to make.'

'You haven't brought your phone out here,' complained Harriet.

'He's a busy man,' Edmund reminded her. 'Come on, let me finish and then you can go in the water. Can you move your legs a little wider apart?'

Harriet continued to stare up at her husband

and suddenly he smiled at her, ran his fingers through her hair and then moved away to sit in the shade, leaving Edmund free to work on her legs.

Slowly Harriet parted her thighs and felt Edmund's hands massaging cream into the tops of her feet, and the place where the skin was stretched tightly over her ankle bones, before moving up over her calf muscles and then, at last, he was rubbing the cool cream into her burning thighs.

Despite herself, Harriet knew that her legs were trembling, and when he spread his fingers wide and eased some of the lotion into the joins of her thighs she was horrified to realise that there was a tightness behind her clitoris, a tightness that always meant the start of her body's ascent to a climax.

Suddenly she rolled sideways off the lounger, nearly falling into the pool in the process. 'That's enough,' she said, her voice just a fraction too high to sound casual, 'I want to swim now.'

Edmund nodded, and Harriet was aware that he knew precisely how she felt and why she'd moved at the moment she did. 'Go ahead,' he agreed. 'Noella, are you going in?'

Noella, who'd been watching the pair through her sunglasses, sat up and put her legs to the ground. 'I'll just dabble my feet in the water,' she announced. 'Harriet can tell me how cold it is.'

As Harriet lowered herself into the pool, Oliver Kesby appeared from the direction of the pitch-and-putt course. He smiled at Noella who raised a hand in greeting.

'Is the pool all right for you?' he asked.

Harriet, who'd just dipped her shoulders beneath the surface, stood upright again, trying to stop her teeth from chattering. 'Fine,' she assured him. 'At least, it should be fine once I start swimming. There's only a problem if you try and keep still.'

'I expect it's warmer where you live,' replied Oliver, eyeing Noella appreciatively. Her large firm breasts were clearly defined beneath the swimsuit and he found her tanned shoulders and limbs highly arousing.

'We heat our pools,' retorted Noella.

Oliver nodded. 'I'd like to, but the cost would be astronomical and not many people holiday in Cornwall these days. They fly off to America, to Disneyland and Orlando.'

'You're blaming us for the cold water are you?' asked Edmund, standing up and removing his slacks.

'Not you personally,' said Oliver hastily.

'Edmund isn't an American!' laughed Noella. 'That's probably the biggest insult you could offer him. Isn't that right, honey?'

But Edmund, who'd dived in and was now moving through the water with a powerful crawl, didn't hear her.

Noella watched him catch up with Harriet in the deep end, and saw the two of them become immersed in a conversation that entailed a great deal of laughter, despite the fact that laughter didn't come easily to her husband. With the slightest of frowns she turned her attention back to Oliver. 'Do you swim?' she asked.

'All the year round, although during the winter months I use the local baths.'

'What else do you do to keep fit?' asked Noella.

His pale blue eyes looked uneasy. 'Oh, you know, a bit of weight-lifting, some karate, that kind of thing.'

'Very macho. How about women?'

'Women?'

'Sure, you know, people like me!'

Oliver's mouth tightened. 'I do know what a woman is.'

'I'm sure you do, honey, and how to treat them. All I meant was, is there a special woman in your life right now?'

'Right now?' he asked, looking at her meaningfully.

'Yeah, right now.'

'There wasn't, until yesterday,' he answered softly.

Noella smiled. 'You know, that was just the answer I was hoping to hear. Where's this little cottage of yours?'

Oliver pointed to a gap between some nearby trees. 'Over there.'

'You in this evening?'

For the first time he looked a little nervous. 'I should be, but . . .'

Noella saw him glance at Edmund, who was

now pulling Harriet around in the water. 'Don't worry about my husband, I can take care of him. Will you be in?'

The temptation was too great for Oliver to resist. He knew that it was a mistake, that this woman and her friends were out of his league, but at this moment the thought of actually touching a woman like Noella, let alone making love to her, was irresistible. 'Yes, I'll be in,' he promised.

'Great, I'll see you later then.' With that Noella lay back on her lounger, put her glasses on again and closed her eyes. After a moment's hesitation, Oliver left them. He had a lot of tidying up to do if Noella was going to keep her word.

In the pool Harriet was laughing as Edmund put his hands on her waist and lifted her in and out of the water. Every time she re-entered the pool she found herself nearer to his body until finally she was actually brushing against him and their legs entwined so that his upper thigh was between hers. 'I want you, Harriet,' he whispered. 'I want to make love to you, to hear you cry out for me the way you cried out for Lewis last night. You know that, don't you?' Harriet nodded, the pressure against her pubic bone was delicious and she didn't want it to stop.

'I'll give you pleasure in ways you've never dreamt of,' he continued, his hands tightening against her bare waist. 'You saw me with Noella in Polperro, didn't you?' Again Harriet nodded. 'Well, I'll take you like that, out in the open where people might come along at any moment. I know you'd enjoy it. I'm right, aren't I?' Again she nodded, feeling the water move against her vulva as their legs trod water together.

'Will you let me?' he persisted, his eyes boring into hers.

'I really shouldn't,' whispered Harriet, her pulse racing. 'What about Lewis?'

Edmund's face darkened. 'Surely you could—'

'Harriet,' Lewis called suddenly, cradling the phone between his chin and shoulder, 'is it all right with you if I go to the local pub and meet up with Mark tonight? I'll only be gone an hour or so.'

'Why can't Mark come here?' asked Harriet, and felt Edmund's fingers dig into her flesh. She realised he thought it was a stupid thing for her to say.

'I didn't think you'd want us working in the house.'

'I really don't care,' retorted Harriet, torn between irritation at the fact that he was willing to go off and leave her alone with Edmund and her desire for him to do exactly that.

Lewis raised his eyebrows and then returned to his phone conversation.

'You see,' said Edmund with a half-smile. 'Fate's been kind to us.'

'There's still Noella,' Harriet pointed out.

'I have a feeling that Noella's been making plans of her own,' said Edmund, who'd already suggested that his wife made her first move towards Oliver in the hope that this would enable him to begin his pursuit of Harriet – a pursuit that he knew Noella anticipated would end with Harriet joining both of them.

Still Harriet hesitated. 'I'm not sure,' she murmured.

'I won't give up,' warned Edmund. 'And believe me, I usually end up getting what I want.'

'Suppose it isn't what I want?' asked Harriet, twisting free of him and starting to swim away.

'But it is, isn't it?' he called after her, and it was.

'You're really going then?' asked Harriet that evening as she watched Lewis taking his jacket from their bedroom wardrobe.

'Sure, you don't mind do you?'

Harriet took a deep breath. 'I don't mind, but I hope you know exactly what you're doing.'

Slinging the jacket over his shoulder he looked thoughtfully at her. 'So do I, Harriet, so do I.'

Harriet knew with absolute certainty that if he went to meet Mark then she and Edmund would make love that evening and the thought both intrigued and frightened her. 'Please, Lewis, don't go,' she said quietly. 'Life's good at the moment, let's not spoil it.'

'I'm not spoiling anything; I'm simply going out for a drink with my scriptwriter. Where's the harm in that?'

She knew then that he was quite determined to have his film scenario acted out, whatever the price, and that once she took the first step, controlling the outcome would prove impossible. 'No harm,' she agreed, turning her back on him to stare out of the window. 'It's strange,' she added as he opened the door and went to leave.

'What's strange?'

'For the first time tonight I understand how Rowena felt that summer we met.'

Lewis's handsome face darkened. 'Don't be ridiculous, this isn't the same thing at all.'

'Yes it is, Lewis, it's exactly the same, except that this time your role is a more passive one. Somehow I think that might prove quite difficult for you to accept.'

'My "role", as you put it, will be as passive as I wish, and no more than that,' he retorted and then he was gone.

In the drawing room Edmund was immersed in a book, but he looked up when Harriet entered. 'Has Lewis gone?'

'Yes. Where's Noella?'

'She told me she was taking a walk – a walk that will, I suspect, lead her straight to Oliver Kesby's cottage.'

'And you don't mind?' enquired Harriet, who was beginning to wonder if all men were as detached as Lewis and Edmund.

'There was a time when I would have minded,' he admitted, 'but that time's past. Tonight I'm rather pleased. Aren't you pleased too?'

Harriet stood awkwardly in the middle of the room, her hands fidgeting at her sides. 'I'm not sure.'

Edmund stood up and crossed the room to her. Placing both hands on her shoulders he smiled into her eyes, but she noticed that there was little warmth in his. 'Come with me,' he murmured. 'In a very short time you'll be as pleased as I am, and that's a promise.'

Taking her by the hand, he led her upstairs and into the bedroom that he and Noella shared. 'Stand quite still,' he said quietly. 'I want to really look at you.'

As Harriet remained motionless he walked round and round her, occasionally pausing to touch a strand of her hair or run his fingerrs up and down her spine. Her body quivered but she kept her breathing even.

'You're really beautiful,' he said at last, and then his fingers began moving over her stomach and hips. Beneath the fabric of her dress her skin seemed to burn. 'Take off your clothes and put this on,' he said abruptly, taking one of his striped shirts off a hanger and handing it to her.

Harriet looked at the shirt. To her amazement, his fingertips caught her nipple with a flick that was almost a caress. Slowly, feeling like someone who'd been hypnotised, she obeyed him.

As she changed, Edmund took off his clothes and when she turned to face him, she saw that he was already fully erect, his penis long and supple.

Reaching forward, he unfastened the top buttons of the shirt so that Harriet's breasts were half-exposed and then stepped back to admire her. 'Perfect,' he exclaimed, and turned her so that she could see herself in the wardrobe mirror. She'd never realised before how sexy a man's shirt looked on a woman, but when he reached round from behind her and plunged a hand down inside the shirt, softly gripping the aching flesh, she closed her eyes for a moment and leant back against him to feel the heat of sexual desire rising off her body.

'Now lie on the bed,' he murmured, 'and I want to cover your eyes.'

Harriet shook her head. 'I don't think so, Edmund. Not until we know each other better.'

He didn't smile, instead his expression was one of keen interest. 'Are you frightened of me?' he asked.

Harriet felt her mouth go dry. 'Not really. Should I be?'

'Perhaps a little, but then I think you are already if the truth be told. Fear's an aphrodisiac, Harriet.'

'I don't want—'

'I know what you want,' he said firmly. 'Now lie back and do as I ask. After all, there's no point in us doing the same things that you do with Lewis, is there? Where's the sense in that? Surely you're with me because you think I can give you something he can't?'

He was speaking the truth, but it was a truth that Harriet was having difficulty in coming to terms with. 'I don't know why I'm with you,' she said defiantly.

'Then let's just assume that I'm right and play it my way, shall we?'

Harriet realised that she had two choices. She could tell Edmund that she'd changed her mind, get up and leave the room and never mention the incident again, or she could stay and discover exactly what it was about him that fascinated her. 'All right,' she agreed after a moment's thought. 'Your way it is.'

'Good girl,' he whispered, and then his hands were on her shoulders and he was pressing her backwards against the bedspread, before taking a black silk scarf from the bedside drawer and tying it carefully over her eyes.

'I want you to lie quite still,' he explained, his voice sounding so remote that for a moment Harriet wondered if he felt anything for her at all, 'and you have to guess what I'm touching you with. All right?'

She frowned. 'I'm not sure I know what you mean.'

'You'll soon find out. Now, thrust your belly upwards.' There was a quaking sensation deep inside Harriet, a mixture of fear and almost terrifying desire. Without a word she arched her back and he watched her slender stomach rise up towards him. With the faintest of smiles, he took a grape from the fruit bowl on the dressing table and, using the palm of his hand, rolled it over the taut exposed flesh.

Harriet gasped at the initial contact. As the small pliable object moved over her straining flesh, she tried to picture it in her mind's eye, but all the time she had to contend with the spirals of desire that its touch was engendering.

'Well, what do you think it is?' asked Edmund, fascinated by the way her top teeth caught on her lower lip when she was concentrating.

'A jelly bean?'

He laughed. 'Now there's an idea for later. No, not a jelly bean, try again.'

'I can't think when you keep moving it around, it feels so good,' murmured Harriet.

'That's what makes the game enjoyable.'

Suddenly Harriet knew the answer. 'A grape.'

'Well done.'

Much to Harriet's dismay he immediately stopped moving the grape over her and she slumped back flat against the bed. He didn't give her any warning as to where she'd be touched next, and when her breasts were suddenly touched by something ice cold, rounded but with hard edges, she gave a low cry of excitement.

The object teased at her swelling tissue, scraping lightly over her rigid nipples until she was squirming helplessly beneath its touch. Edmund couldn't resist letting his spare hand stroke down Harriet's side, and then, as the object dipped beneath the underside of one breast, he allowed the roaming hand to stray to the join of her inner thigh. Harriet's legs parted automatically and her entire vulva seemed to pulsate with need.

'What is it?' he whispered, and Harriet tried to

blot out the hand at the top of her leg and concentrate on the object now tracing the outline of her left breast. She wished that she had a firmer grasp of its shape but that seemed to change, sometimes flat and sometimes concave, and she was totally confused.

'It's some kind of metal,' she gasped, her hips wriggling at the feelings that were spreading through her pelvis.

'That's right, it's metal.' Again he let his free hand move, but this time the fingers parted her pubic hair and she felt the touch of his fingertip against the edge of her outer sex lips – a touch so gentle and yet so precise that it could have been that of a surgeon.

'Please, press harder there,' she moaned, finding the teasing torment almost unbearable.

'When you guess the object,' he repeated and continued the tender stroking movement.

'It's cutlery!' shouted Harriet as the edge of the object became clearer to her. 'A spoon, isn't it?'

'What size spoon?' he teased, his own excitement growing with her increasing need.

'That's not fair.'

'I make the rules tonight! What size?'

'A dessertspoon.'

'Quite right, a dessertspoon. Now I'm going to use something on you that might have some kind of connection with a dessertspoon. Don't move, I just have to go and fetch it.'

Harriet could have moved, could have taken off her blindfold or simply flexed all her tense muscles, but she obeyed him because she realised that every move he made was calculated to ensure that she had the maximum amount of pleasure from the final climax.

Edmund came back into the room so quietly that she didn't hear him and it was only when she felt her sex lips being parted that she realised he was back. 'Now, tell me what this is,' he urged her, and suddenly the aching space where she longed to feel his penis was filled instead by a freezing cold substance that had no sooner touched her burning tissue than it began to melt and trickle down her shamelessly spread thighs.

'It's ice-cream!' she shouted, ecstatic at both the sensation and the ease of the test.

'I'm afraid it isn't,' said Edmund in mock regret, but before she could protest she felt a new sensation between her thighs. It was the tip of his tongue, and it moved slowly up her inner channel until it reached the substance, and once there it began to lick it away, at the same time adding further torture to her highly stimulated nerve endings.

Edmund used both his hands to hold Harriet's outer sex lips apart as he consumed the substance that was now almost melted. Once he'd cleared it away he allowed his tongue to enter her most secret place, the place he had been longing to see from the moment he'd first met her.

His tongue was long and rougher than she was used to, but felt to the writhing Harriet to be made of velvet. When he probed inside the entrance to her vagina, and then curled his tongue upwards, he spread the last drops of the substance against the top wall of her vagina, around the area of the G-spot. The highly sensitive gland immediately responded by sending urgent streaks of red-hot pleasure up through her pubic bone and she clenched her buttocks in order to heighten the feelings.

'Guess again,' said Edmund softly. 'Guess right and I'll let you come, Harriet, and that's what you need to do now, isn't it? I can tell by the way you're so tight. Tell me, do you ache here?' and he put a hand across the base of her belly, pressing down so that the ache he'd mentioned increased and she was sure her climax would be triggered.

'Yes! Yes, I do!' she screamed, no longer caring if anyone heard. 'I don't know what it is. Just let me come before I go mad.'

He laughed softly. 'You won't go mad, Harriet, except with pleasure. You're nearly right, but what do Americans like almost as much as ice-cream?'

She knew, but couldn't think of the word, and all the time she tried to recall it he kept his tongue moving and his hand pressing against her until it felt as though the whole of her lower body was on fire, as she tried to force the elusive orgasm past the point of no return.

Seeing her straining and hearing her gasps and pleas, Edmund too had difficulty in controlling himself and at last he put her out of her misery. 'In England it's more usually eaten unfrozen,' he murmured.

'Yoghurt!' shouted Harriet. 'It's frozen yoghurt.'

'Yes, it is. So, what would you like as your reward?'

Harriet was almost sobbing now, desperate for the blissful moment of release. 'You know what I want,' she cried.

'I want to hear you say it, Harriet. I want you to beg.'

'I want a climax, and I can't wait, I just can't!' she cried. With a sigh of regret Edmund finally gave in to her pleading. He continued to lick at her G-spot, one hand remaining on her lower belly, using his other hand to touch her very lightly on the area surrounding her clitoris.

'Bear down for me, Harriet,' he urged her. 'I want to see the little nub at the moment you come.'

She didn't understand what he meant, but she heard the words and pressed down internally, forcing her clitoris to emerge from beneath its hood. Then Edmund moved his mouth and, with an almost imperceptible touch, he swept the ice cold tip of his tongue over the exposed bunch of nerve endings.

For Harriet it was a moment of ecstasy so intense that she wasn't sure she could bear it. Shards of shattering pleasure ripped through her, and the moment her body began to come down from the pinnacle of its pleasure, Edmund told her to bear down again and he repeated the touch, so that once more every nerve ending in her body was activated. This time she screamed at the top of her voice and her body heaved from side to side forcing Edmund to release her and sit on the bed, watching as she was racked by the second and final convulsion that signalled her total release and respite from the torture of prolonged sexual tension.

Edmund was both relieved and delighted by her responses. She was all that he'd imagined and more. With Noella he sometimes had the feeling that she agreed to his games and experiments to please him rather than to please herself. With Harriet there would be no such fear because Harriet wasn't his wife. He felt reasonably certain that she'd allow him to remain the controller, a role he relished, but only if he made the rewards great enough. The fact that his hold over her would be so tenuous was an aphrodisiac in itself, because he had a contradictory streak in him that meant he liked to control sexually, but only strong-willed women. He gained no satisfaction from exerting control over naturally passive women. And he knew that he was still searching for the perfect soul mate, a woman who could be everything to him. Watching Harriet as she revelled in their activities, he wondered if it was possible that she could be the one. If so, he would have to take her away from Lewis and that, he knew, would be extremely difficult as well as ultimately dangerous. Lewis was not a man to cross, either personally or professionally.

Harriet opened her eyes and stared up at this

man she'd just allowed to pleasure her so thoroughly. 'Is that all?' she asked, her voice soft and languid. 'What about you?'

She expected him to smile, but smiles were difficult for Edmund and he merely nodded thoughtfully, as though in appreciation of her words. She couldn't help contrasting his behaviour with Lewis's warm, caring way of making love, but even so still felt a longing to have Edmund deep inside her. That way, she was sure, she could force him into giving more of himself emotionally than he was at the moment. Quite apart from that, she needed to have him fill her, to satisfy her need for closer contact between them.

'I think I'll save something for another time,' he said slowly.

'You mean, you're not going to make love to me?'

'I've done that, or have you forgotten already?'

'Hardly,' laughed Harriet, moving her still-heavy limbs slowly on the bed. 'But there's more to sex than that.'

'Yes, much more, and we've got six weeks to explore the boundaries. I think, though, that there is something I'd like to do before we finish tonight.'

Harriet moved over on the bed as he lay down beside her. His hands drew her over him until she was crouching on all fours, her hands resting on either side of his waist so that her breasts brushed against his belly and his erection nestled between them. Edmund lifted his hands and wrapped her swollen breasts around the shaft of his penis, giving a small sigh of pleasure at the moment of contact. 'Now move your body for me,' he murmured.

Harriet looked down at his face, still apparently unmoved by what was happening, and she felt an urgent desire to force some kind of response from him. Slowly she moved her body rhythmically up and down, taking care to linger at the top of each upward movement so that the purple glans was given maximum stimulation. Then, once her rhythm was established and Edmund's eyes started to cloud with excitement, she moved more slowly and heard his breath catch in his throat as he lost his momentum and his climax, which had been imminent, started to fade.

'My turn to play teasing games,' laughed Harriet, but to her surprise Edmund didn't laugh back; instead he simply stared at her, his soft brown eyes totally without expression.

'Isn't it more fun this way?' she whispered, slowing down again as his breathing began to quicken. Edmund swallowed hard, and she felt his hips begin to move as he started to force the pace himself, no longer allowing her to dictate the game.

Harriet began to lift her body away from his but Edmund was too quick for her and his hands gripped her tightly. His strength was startling and suddenly she was moving as he wanted, out of her control. Within seconds his mouth twisted in a grimace of ecstasy as he felt the tingling in his glans increase in intensity, his semen rushing upwards, and with a half-choked groan he finally came, his seed spilling out of him with immense force and falling across the surfaces of Harriet's breasts and onto his stomach.

Now, relaxed and sated, his eyes grew warm and for the first time he smiled at Harriet. 'That was very interesting,' he said softly. 'I can tell that we're going to have some wonderful times together.'

'Why wouldn't you come inside me?' asked Harriet, rolling over to lie beside him.

He shifted away a little so that only their shoulders were touching. 'Because I wanted it too much. I prefer to delay the ultimate pleasure for as long as possible, and there'll be other times, won't there Harriet?'

Lying beside him, feeling incredibly alive and energetic, Harriet made a sound that was half-pleasure and half-regret.

'Yes, Edmund,' she agreed. 'There will be other times.'

'Let me get this right,' said Mark, leaning back in his chair. 'The heroine of *Dark Secret*, Helena, is now happily married but starts an affair with one of her husband's closest friends. An affair that the husband is aware of but allows to continue?'

Lewis drained his glass and wished he'd stayed at home. 'No, that's not right,' he said irritably. 'Honest to God, Mark, there are times when I wonder how you ever manage to get a script together.'

'It's certainly not easy when I'm working with you,' conceded Mark.

'The whole point of this film is that the husband is aware of the *possibility* of an affair between Helena and his friend. Let's be honest, she isn't the type of young woman who's going to be your average wife, is she?'

'No, but since she's madly in love with her husband I don't think an affair's very likely. Sure, I can understand the husband being a bit paranoid, you know – thinking every guy he meets wants her and all that – but would she really start something so soon after her wedding?'

'I've no idea.'

Mark stared at him. 'You must have, because if she doesn't have an affair then you haven't got a story.'

'Right.'

'What do you mean, "right"?'

'I mean that if an affair doesn't materialise then the story's useless and we have to think of another.'

Mark had a sinking sensation in his stomach. 'Lew, this is not a good idea.'

Lewis frowned. 'How do you mean?'

'You're playing games with other people's lives again. You were lucky with *Dark Secret*, it worked out the way you wanted it to in the end, but this time you might not be as fortunate.'

'How do you know what I wanted last time?'

'Believe me, Lew, if anyone knows you I do and you were better off without Rowena, but Harriet's a very different matter. If you lose Harriet you'll regret it for the rest of your life.'

'If I lose Harriet it won't be my fault,' said Lewis through clenched teeth. 'All I want to do is explore how people react to forbidden desires. It's always seemed to me that by putting something out of bounds you actually create a greater need for that commodity, whether it's sex or anything else. If someone said to our heroine: "go right ahead, have a passionate affair with your husband's best friend, no one will get hurt, no one will mind and you'll walk away at the end unscathed" then she probably wouldn't bother to try. It's the fact that it's forbidden, that it holds the potential for disaster, that makes it so irresistible to her.'

'And to her husband,' said Mark dryly.

Lewis nodded. 'Yes, and to her husband. The potential for disaster is so great that he can't help himself. He has to test his power over that of his friend. Pathetically macho really.'

Mark cleared his throat. 'Lew, why make this *cinéma vérité*? Why don't you just let me draft a script and then make some alterations if you don't like it? Most people make films that way, you know. They didn't set up a phone-in and follow up the results when they made *Sleepless in Seattle*.'

'My films are different, that's why they're so successful. I'm not willing to change a winning formula.'

'What about the other characters' desires? Have you taken them into account?'

'As much as I can, but again it's something that you have to see in order to understand.'

Mark shrugged, realising nothing would make Lewis change his mind. 'You're the boss. So, when do I start?'

Lewis looked at his watch. 'I imagine you could probably start now! No, seriously – I'm not sure but I'll give you a call tomorrow and let you know for definite if the project's on.'

'You mean you'll know by then?'

'Yes,' said Lewis, picking up their glasses and making his way to the bar for refills. 'I'll know for sure by the morning.'

Chapter Five

WHEN HARRIET OPENED her eyes the next morning she found Lewis propped up on one elbow looking down at her with an expression of great tenderness in his eyes. She remembered then that she'd been woken when he'd arrived back at Penruan, but had feigned sleep when he'd reached for her in the comfort of their double bed.

'You always look deliciously tempting first thing in the morning!' he teased, kissing her softly on the lips. Harriet smiled and her arms went automatically round his neck so that she could return the kiss, but with more passion. It was only when his hands began roaming over her body, cupping her breasts and straying between her thighs that she remembered the way Edmund had tormented her with such consummate skill the previous evening, and her body stiffened.

Lewis felt her reaction and very slowly he released her so that she was lying back looking up

99

at him, without the distraction of his touch. 'The game's begun then?' he queried softly.

Harriet felt herself colouring but was unable to look away from him, or to lie. 'Yes, the game's begun,' she murmured.

Lewis was shocked by the sudden naked fury that surged through him, and Harriet was equally shocked by the expression of rage in his eyes. 'It's what you wanted,' she reminded him. 'At least your film now has a beginning.'

Lewis tried to calm himself, knowing that she was right and his behaviour was ridiculous. This was why he'd gone out, leaving her behind with Edmund. This was necessary for the whole project to get off the ground, and he'd expected to feel a frisson of excitement, but at that moment all he felt was a desire to hit Edmund and then return to America, taking Harriet with him.

'It's not too late to stop it,' said Harriet. 'If you like I . . .'

Lewis shook his head. 'There's no question of stopping it. Now that you've chosen to begin we have to see it through, for both our sakes.'

'That's not true,' said Harriet. 'I don't need to see it through. You're the one who wants that, because your film needs an ending as well as a beginning.'

'You mean you're not interested in discovering where this will lead you?' queried Lewis. 'Come on, Harriet, that isn't like you. If Edmund's appeal is great enough to draw you into his bed then surely you want to find out if it's great enough to keep you at his side.'

100

'I'm not interested in being at his side!' she exclaimed.

'How sad for Edmund. I wonder if he knows it's just his body you're interested in,' mused Lewis.

'All right,' said Harriet, sitting up in bed and letting the sheet fall away from her so that Lewis could see her bare breasts and the soft creamy skin of her shoulders and back. 'Yes, I do want to "see this through" as you put it. I want to find out what kind of a man Edmund is, and whether my desire for him increases or decreases as I get to know him better. Does that satisfy you?'

'At least it's honest,' remarked Lewis. 'I take it last night was a success?'

'Yes, a great success.'

Lewis grabbed hold of Harriet's arms and pulled her on top of him, easing her down on his painfully hard erection. 'Then I hope this doesn't prove a disappointment,' he said tightly, as he moved her up and down with his powerful arms.

Feeling the first flush of arousal beginning to smoulder in her belly, Harriet knew that it wouldn't be, and a few minutes later she was lost in the familiar pleasure that Lewis could always give her. When, about ten minutes later, she gave a cry of ecstasy, Edmund, already awake on the other side of the bedroom wall, clenched his fists at his sides and tried not to think about what was happening.

At breakfast only Noella seemed cheerful. She chattered on about how she wanted to visit the

101

Paul Corin Magnificent Music Machines collection that was kept in the family mill beside the River Looe. 'They've got a 20-foot Belgian dance hall organ!' she exclaimed, looking through the leaflet that she'd found on the hall table.

'I'd have thought you'd seen more than your share of organs,' laughed Lewis.

Noella gave him a sideways glance. 'I'm always anxious to extend my experiences, honey.'

Lewis nodded. 'So I've heard. I saw young Oliver a few minutes ago when I went to fetch the mail. He looked a little tired I thought. Too much working out perhaps?'

Noella laughed. 'He'll soon pick up; strong young men of his age have wonderful stamina.'

Harriet looked across the kitchen table at Noella. 'Did you really go and see him last night?'

'Sure, and it was great. Not shocked are you?'

'No, of course not, it's just that you hardly know him.'

'Hell, I don't *know* Edmund after ten years of marriage,' said Noella. 'Do you honestly think you know Lewis?'

'I suppose not.'

'There you are then, what's the difference?'

'Nearly ten years,' said Lewis with a grin.

At that moment the telephone rang and Harriet went to answer it. To her delighted surprise it was Ella calling from London, but sounding rather subdued.

'I just got your letter, Harriet,' she said, talking more rapidly than normal. 'Do you really mean it, about me coming to stay?'

'Of course I do. Lewis would like to meet you as well.'

'The thing is, I've got to quit my flat. I'm broke and right now there's no work in sight.'

'Then come straight away,' Harriet urged her. She lowered her voice. 'Quite honestly, Ella, I'd love to have a friend here. It's all a bit complicated and if you were with us I think it would be easier.'

'In what way, complicated? You're on your honeymoon aren't you?' At the prospect of some kind of intrigue, Ella's voice had immediately brightened.

'Yes, and I can't explain, but I need you here to keep my feet on the ground. I'm in serious danger of going out of control.'

'Not you, Harriet. You're the most balanced person I've ever met.'

Harriet gave a short laugh. 'That was a long time ago, Ella. Believe me, I've changed. Look, when can you come down?'

'Today if you like,' responded Ella. 'I'll drive myself but I doubt if I'll be with you until late this evening.'

'That'll be great!' enthused Harriet. 'And you can stay for the whole six weeks if you like,' she added recklessly.

After Ella had thanked her profusely, Harriet replaced the receiver and went back into the kitchen where Noella and Lewis were deep in conversation. They drew apart when she entered, but for a moment she'd been certain that she'd seen Lewis's hand on the nape of Noella's neck.

'Who was it?' asked Lewis.

'Ella; she's coming down today.'

He pulled a face. 'She doesn't waste any time.'

'You'll like her,' Harriet assured him. 'She's really pretty, and an actress as well so you'll have plenty to talk about.'

'In my experience, actresses only like to talk about themselves. Are you coming to look at these organs that are fascinating Noella, or are you staying behind with Edmund?'

Harriet shook her head. 'I'll come with you two.'

Lewis hoped that his relief didn't show in his eyes.

Once again it was Lewis who drove them through the winding narrow Cornish roads. Harriet hated driving when he was a passenger, he was always giving her instructions, and Noella flatly refused to tackle driving on the left-hand side of the road.

As they walked round the display, which Lewis found totally engrossing, the two women were left on their own to study the various organs. 'What did you think of Edmund as a lover?' asked Noella beneath her breath as a young couple stood next to them, studying the same instrument.

Harriet turned her head sharply to stare at the other woman. 'What do you mean?'

'I mean did you think he was a good lover?'

'Ssh!' said Harriet.

'Well, you must have an opinion and I'd like to hear it,' said Noella, lowering her voice a little but smiling broadly.

'Did he tell you about us?' asked Harriet, shocked at the idea.

'Of course not; Edmund never tells me anything,' lied Noella. 'I knew though. I always know when he's started an affair; he gets this satisfied look, like a cat that's had the cream.'

Harriet wasn't sure whether to believe Noella or not, but to her surprise she felt a strange excitement discussing Edmund with his own wife. 'As a matter of fact I thought he was an incredible lover,' she said calmly.

'Better than Lewis?'

Harriet shook her head. 'No, not better, but different.'

Noella nodded. 'I can imagine he would be. Edmund's different from most men. At times he goes too far.'

'In what way?' asked Harriet.

'You'll find out – if you continue the affair that is. Oliver was incredible too,' she added.

'Better than Edmund?' laughed Harriet.

'Not better, but *very* different! Well, to tell the truth, he was more my style,' admitted Noella. 'The problem is that Edmund likes to make things very complicated, but I just like to get on with things. Oliver was about as basic as I'd want to get, but he was exactly what I needed last night. I might have to teach him a few refinements before the holiday's over I suppose, although too many and I'll have spoilt him.'

'So what kind of sex did you have?' asked Harriet, unable to resist learning more.

'The instant kind. He stood against the wall, lifted me up and took me like that, without even kissing me. Then we had a bath together and he took me from behind in the water, and finally we did it in his back garden, although the midges were a bit of a problem.'

'I don't think you're telling me the truth,' laughed Harriet.

'Why not? He's young and strong, three times was nothing to him.'

'Well, it doesn't sound my kind of thing,' said Harriet firmly. 'I like the more sophisticated approach.'

'Wouldn't you like to see him in action?' asked Noella.

'Of course not.'

'You don't find watching turns you on?'

Harriet remembered watching Rowena once, a long time ago, and recalled the tremendous sexual excitement she'd experienced as she observed her. 'Yes,' she admitted.

'Then come and watch us through one of the windows next time I go over there.'

'No thanks,' said Harriet. 'Oliver really doesn't interest me.'

'That's a pity. I must say, the idea of you and Edmund together interests me,' said Noella thoughtfully.

'Meaning what?'

'That I'd like the opportunity to see the pair of you in action.'

'I'm surprised you don't suggest we have a foursome,' said Harriet sharply, before turning on her heel and going over to join Lewis.

'That's just what I intend to have, honey,' whispered Noella to herself, but she knew better than to say as much at this stage of the game.

Standing next to her husband, Harriet wished that Noella knew what she knew: that they were all pawns in an elaborate plot thought up by Lewis to provide him with material for his new film. If she did, she might not be quite so keen to tell Harriet everything she was thinking and doing, because Harriet, despite her reservations about the film, knew that she must pass on all that Noella had told her to Lewis, in order for the film to be a truthful reflection of the way events unfolded.

The three of them had a pub lunch on their way back, and it was gone four before they arrived at Penruan House. Edmund was lying on one of the loungers by the poolside, and Noella gave a squeal of horror. 'He isn't wearing a hat or sunblock!' she complained.

'We're not quite so sun-conscious as you are in America,' admitted Harriet. 'I think it's because we get so little really hot weather in England that we hate to waste it.'

'But it's more dangerous if you just lie in it occasionally.'

'Most Englishmen wouldn't be seen dead

covered with sunblock,' laughed Harriet. 'Unless they were part of our national cricket team that is.'

'Does that mean you think Edmund's right?' asked Lewis, slamming the driver's door with what Noella considered unnecessary force.

'Not Edmund particularly.'

'The English then? Are you saying that the English have more sense than the rest of the civilised world when it comes to lying in the glare of the sun and frying themselves?'

Harriet looked at him in surprise. 'No, of course not. I was simply explaining to Noella why it was that Edmund wasn't covered from head to foot with protection.'

'We must remember, Noella, that America was once a colony that belonged to this country,' said Lewis, with barely suppressed irritation. 'It's strange, but I've noticed that no matter where the English choose to live, in later life they still maintain illusions of superiority based purely on the fact that they're British!'

'Look, what is this?' asked Harriet. 'I wasn't talking about superiority, I know it's stupid to sunbathe without protection. All I was saying was—'

'They also stick together,' interrupted Lewis. 'And they have an uncanny ability to exclude other people from this elite British Club.'

Harriet couldn't believe what she was hearing, and even Noella was taken aback by the anger in Lewis's voice. 'Hey, no big deal,' she assured him.

'If Edmund burns it's his fault. Not that he will burn,' she added. 'He never does, worse luck!'

'Personally I could do with a drink,' said Lewis shortly, and he made his way into the house.

'What was all that about?' asked Noella.

Harriet shrugged. 'I've no idea.'

'Could it be that the famous Lewis James is feeling jealous?'

Harriet knew that Noella was right, but she laughed lightly and began to walk over to Edmund. 'Hardly, he doesn't know he's got any reason to feel jealous.'

'It's what they call instinct, honey. I should watch your step if I were you. He's gorgeous when he's angry though, isn't he?'

'Not to me,' said Harriet, furious with Lewis for behaving like that when he was the one who'd pushed her and Edmund together, and had urged her to follow her desires.

At the sound of the women's voices Edmund sat up, stretched his arms above his head and then glanced at his watch. 'You took your time.'

'We had lunch in an incredible little pub,' explained Noella, 'and then Lewis brought us back via the scenic route.'

'Actually I think he got lost,' said Harriet tartly.

Edmund gave a short laugh. 'Did he admit it?'

'No,' said Harriet, 'but he isn't a great one for admitting his mistakes.'

'Lewis is in a bad mood,' confided Noella, sitting on the arm of her husband's lounger while Harriet sat on the grass.

Edmund reached down and stroked the top of Harriet's head. 'What's he in a mood about? The film?'

'In a way,' said Harriet.

Edmund's eyes narrowed but he didn't respond. Instead he leant forward and cupped his hands round the back of Harriet's head before very gently moving it from side to side. 'Just relax into my hands,' he murmured. 'This is good for tension.'

'I'm not tense,' she protested, but she knew that she was. Lewis's outburst had unsettled her more than she'd realised.

As Edmund rocked her head she felt her shoulders relax and her head seemed to become heavier and heavier as she gradually let his hands take its full weight. Once she was totally relaxed, he nodded at Noella who brushed the back of her hand softly up the outside of Harriet's bare arm. Harriet knew that it was Noella's hand and not Edmund's, but surprisingly she didn't mind. With her eyes closed and the soft warmth of the late afternoon sun shining down on her, it just felt wonderfully reassuring to have them both touching and soothing her in what seemed, at first, to be a totally non-sexual way.

Slowly, though, the sensations changed. Edmund let her head rest against his knees and used his hands to work at the bunched shoulder muscles, slipping his fingers gradually lower beneath the back of her sundress, while Noella's hand moved higher to caress the flesh of her highly sensitive upper arm, tracing the outline of her cutaway sleeve.

Harriet felt her body begin to awaken. Her skin tingled and the sleepy languor that she'd been experiencing changed into a heightened awareness of her body, an awareness that brought with it a longing for some more intimate kind of contact.

Her breathing grew more shallow and Edmund, watching her from beneath lowered lids, had just started to move his hands round to the front of her dress when he saw Lewis coming across the grass to join them. Without hurrying, he changed position and by the time Lewis arrived, Edmund was once again cradling Harriet's skull while Noella was sitting with her arm round her husband's shoulders.

Feeling them withdrawing from her, Harriet opened her eyes and saw Lewis standing over her. He was blocking out the sun and suddenly she felt cold – cold and frightened. The fear was hard to define, but then she realised what it was; it was fear of losing him, and all the warmth he'd brought into her life.

'How about a swim?' suggested Lewis.

Harriet saw that he was already wearing his trunks. 'I haven't brought my costume,' she said. 'I'll go and get it from the house.'

'You don't need a costume. I'm sure Edmund, being a true English gentleman, will close his eyes while you strip off if you're feeling shy.'

Harriet didn't know what to do, or what Lewis

wanted her to do. She tried to read the expression in his eyes but it was impossible, and so she decided that since he'd placed her in this position she'd do whatever she wanted. To her surprise, what she wanted was to take off all her clothes in front of both Edmund and Noella and then swim in the cool water with Lewis while they watched.

'I don't mind if they don't,' she said with a smile and Lewis watched her stand up and unbutton her dress, easing it down over her naked breasts, before tugging it across her hips and then letting it fall to the grass and stepping out of it. Her pink bikini pants were removed just as rapidly and within seconds she was standing naked before them all.

Lewis glanced at Edmund to see how he was reacting, and was surprised by the look of naked hunger on the other man's face. Clearly he'd been right about Edmund, he thought. He desired Harriet, and their sexual encounter last night appeared to have fuelled rather than lessened this desire. Surprisingly, considering how this would add to the interest of the plot, Lewis felt little satisfaction.

Noella, who personally found Harriet too slender for her taste but who appreciated a beautiful body on purely aesthetic grounds, was also less than delighted by the expression on Edmund's face. It was more complex than lust and carried a suggestion of deeper emotions, although he was a man who normally kept his emotions very much to himself.

Harriet was astonished to find herself revelling in the attention. She could feel the tension between the two men, and sensed Noella's anxiety as well as her interest, but any trace of shyness vanished the moment all her clothes were shed and she could hardly wait to enter the pool with Lewis while Edmund sat watching her, remembering the previous night.

Lewis got in the pool first and then stood waist deep in the water holding his arms up to his wife. Harriet looked back over her shoulder at Edmund, saw that he was still watching her intently, and jumped into the temporary safety of Lewis's embrace.

'You're enjoying this, aren't you?' he whispered as they swam up the pool. 'Did you expect to feel like this when you were with both of us?'

Harriet shook her head. 'No, I thought I'd feel awkward or ashamed.'

He smiled with a look of satisfaction. 'You see where forbidden desires can lead you. Tread water for a moment, I'm just taking my trunks off.'

Harriet did as he said and, while he was taking off his trunks and letting them fall to the bottom of the pool, she looked across at Edmund and Noella and waved cheerfully. 'It's lovely and warm,' she shouted.

'I'm quite warm here,' said Edmund dryly.

Harriet laughed. 'You're sure you don't want to join us?'

Suddenly Lewis's hands were hard on her waist. 'Don't even suggest it' he said fiercely.

'This is for us, and us alone. Wrap your legs round my waist now.'

Her legs lifted easily in the water and the upper half of her torso tilted back a little as she wrapped her legs around his waist. He then pushed her backwards through the water until she reached the edge of the pool, and once she had something solid behind her he put his hands over her shoulders until they were resting on the poolside, easing his body towards hers so that she could feel his erection nudging at her outer sex lips.

'Touch your breasts,' he whispered. 'Make your nipples hard so that I can suck on them while I enter you.'

'I can't,' said Harriet. 'The other two will notice.'

'No they won't.'

'They will!'

Lewis stared at her. 'Does that really bother you? Wouldn't you like Edmund to see us making love? Doesn't the thought of him having to watch me possess you, when that's what he wants to do, excite you?'

It did. Already, without even touching herself, Harriet's nipples were hardening and she was twisting her lower body in the water, wriggling with rising desire. 'Yes,' she admitted, her pupils dilating with desire.

'Touch them then, roll them between your fingers and pull on them very gently, the way you like me to.'

Harriet's excitement was so great now that she

could hardly breathe and her fingers moved quickly to her breasts, clearly visible above the waterline. As she pinched at the rigid pink tips, flickers of sexual excitement darted through her and she felt a heaviness between her thighs that was accentuated by the feeling of the water against her vulva.

Lewis's dark eyes seemed to turn black as he watched her, and once her nipples were standing out in rigid peaks, he lowered his head and began to suck on each of them in turn while Harriet squirmed helplessly in the water longing for his penis, that was now brushing against her thigh, to penetrate her.

From his seat by the poolside, Edmund watched in total silence. Noella was leaning forward, her excitement undisguised, but Edmund remained externally impassive. Inside it was another story. He couldn't remember when he'd last felt so aroused and so helpless. Harriet was Lewis's wife, and as such they could make love wherever they chose, whereas he had to sit and wait for another opportunity to have that glorious body straining beneath his ministrations.

Harriet was enjoying herself too, he knew that. Enjoying both the physical sensations Lewis was arousing and the knowledge that Edmund was watching. He didn't have to watch, he could easily turn away or return to the house, but it was impossible. He needed to sit and see it through, and as Lewis's movements in the pool caused the water to lap against the sides, Edmund knew that he'd get his revenge. Next time he was with Harriet he'd make her pay, pay in the most deliciously exciting way, for putting him through this torture.

When Lewis finally entered her, Harriet gave a tiny gasp at the force of his initial thrust. Then he was rotating his hips, brushing against the most sensitive part of her vagina just inside the entrance, and she felt her muscles tightening inexorably as her climax approached.

Lewis felt her internal muscles start to spasm around him, and he nipped lightly at the soft skin at the top of her breast as the tingling at the tip of his penis extended down the shaft and his body bunched itself in readiness for release.

Harriet was about to come, he knew that from the way her head had gone back and the tendons of her neck were taut with tension. Quickly he changed his rhythm, thrusting harder and deeper in order to increase his own stimulation. All the time, Harriet's body felt as though it was expanding until at last the pleasure spread through her entire body, making even her hands and feet tingle in the final moments of ecstasy.

Lewis came only a few seconds after her, his hips pumping in the water, and as he shuddered violently he let go of the poolside and gripped Harriet's body tightly, pulling her against him and staring directly into her eyes until he was finally spent.

Trembling violently Harriet clung to him, resting her head against his shoulder as she

116

recovered, while Edmund and Noella continued to watch. Looking over his wife's head, Lewis caught Edmund's eye and for a moment the two men stared at each other. Then, surprisingly, Edmund smiled one of his rare smiles before getting to his feet and walking back to the house. The smile should have comforted Lewis, but it didn't.

Now that the excitement of the moment was over, Harriet felt embarrassed and she was relieved to see that Edmund had gone. Climbing out of the pool, she let Lewis wrap her in a towel and then rub her dry while Noella pulled her lounger into a shaded area and closed her eyes.

'Nice?' asked Lewis with a grin.

Harriet sighed. 'Very nice. Lewis, I don't need anyone but you.'

'I'm sure if you tell Edmund that, he'll accept it. I don't imagine he's ever forced his attentions on a woman.'

'I can't,' admitted Harriet after a pause.

Lewis's hands slowed on the towel. 'Why not?'

'I want to know more.'

'More about what?'

She sighed. 'I don't know how to explain this, but Edmund gives the impression that he knows things other people don't, things that I want to know about as well.'

'Dangerous things?' enquired Lewis.

'Perhaps.'

'That should add to the film's box office appeal,' he said with what appeared to be satisfaction. When Harriet shivered he resumed his brisk towelling of her body.

'It isn't love,' she murmured.

'No, of course not,' said Lewis, handing her the discarded dress. 'I never thought that it would be, at least not yet.'

Harriet looked at him in dismay. 'You can't believe it will turn into love?'

'Why can't I?'

'Well, if you did you wouldn't risk playing the game, would you?'

'I'm not playing a game, I'm writing a film,' he said patiently.

'And you're willing to risk me falling in love with Edmund?' Her voice was rising and in the distance Noella stirred.

'I can't control your feelings Harriet. If you're going to fall in love with someone else it might as well be now than later on in our marriage.'

'I don't want to love him!' she said angrily.

'Good, then I'm sure you won't. Personally I'd say that Edmund would be very hard to love, since love is essentially a two way thing and he doesn't seem to me to be capable of loving a woman back.'

'That's all right then,' said Harriet.

'I want to know exactly what he does to you,' Lewis murmured as he rolled up the wet towel. 'I want you to tell me all the details every time.'

'And if I won't?'

'I'll find out in other ways,' was all he would say, but Harriet guessed that, just as he had for *Dark Secret*, he'd use concealed cameras.

'You might have to use other ways,' she retorted. 'I don't think I want to talk to you about what we do.'

'Fine.'

'Time for a bath, I think,' said Noella, getting out of her chair and strolling towards them. 'You both look very serious. Not a lover's tiff surely? Not after such a nice swim together!'

'We're just tired,' said Harriet shortly, and she went into the house ahead of the other two.

'What are you playing at, Lewis?' asked Noella.

He smiled at her, and once again she wished that she was more his type, because she knew that he'd be the most incredible lover. 'I'm not playing at anything,' he said innocently. 'I'm merely having a quiet honeymoon.'

'You're never quiet, and this is the strangest honeymoon I've ever heard of,' she said briskly. 'No, you're up to something. I just can't work out what it is.'

'Don't try, Noella, you'd be wasting your time.'

'You mean I'm not bright enough to work it out?'

Lewis shook his head. 'I mean there's nothing to know.'

'I know when someone's lying to me!' she laughed. 'Hey, there's Oliver. I'll go and have a word with him and then run that bath I mentioned. Care to share it with me?'

'I'll take a rain check!' laughed Lewis.

Harriet, feeling surprisingly low considering the episode in the pool, walked into the drawing room, sat down in one of the armchairs and gave a small sigh.

'What's wrong?' asked Edmund.

Harriet jumped. She hadn't seen him hidden in the depths of the other chair. 'Nothing, I'm tired that's all.'

'I didn't like watching you and Lewis in the pool,' said Edmund quietly. 'In fact, I positively disliked it.'

'You didn't have to watch.'

Edmund smiled to himself. 'But you wanted me to watch, Harriet. Isn't that true?'

'It didn't matter to me,' she lied.

'When we're next together, I'm afraid I shall have to make you pay for what you did to me,' he murmured.

A tingle of excitement ran up Harriet's spine but before she could reply Lewis and Noella joined them and she was left to think about what he'd said. She knew that he hadn't been joking because he wasn't the kind of man who made jokes, and after Noella's warning she wondered if perhaps she would be wiser not to carry on their affair. Wiser certainly, but if she didn't carry on then she'd never learn what it was she wanted to learn: the extent to which Edmund took his women in the course of making love to them.

Chapter Six

THEY WERE JUST finishing their meal that evening when the front doorbell rang. 'It must be Ella!' exclaimed Harriet, starting to rise from her chair.

'I'll go,' said Lewis. 'You haven't finished the famous shepherds' pie yet. Is there any over for your friend if she's hungry?'

'There's plenty,' Noella assured him. 'I hardly touched mine. I'm afraid it's one English delicacy I can do without.'

'Be nice to her, Lewis,' said Harriet as he left the room.

'How nice do you want him to be?' enquired Noella.

'Polite will be sufficient,' laughed Harriet. 'I'm afraid Lewis isn't that keen on having her here at all, although I really can't imagine why.'

At that moment, having opened the front door and found himself face to face with Ella Walker,

Lewis couldn't imagine why he hadn't wanted her to come either. She was shorter than Harriet and slim with fair shoulder-length hair and amazing deep blue eyes that seemed to hold a vast amount of knowledge in their depths. When she raised her eyes to smile at him, he felt a flicker of desire and realised that this was a young woman who knew the power of her own sexuality and how to use it to good purpose. He didn't mind that, in fact he admired it, but he was surprised. Somehow he'd pictured Ella as a far more passive girl.

She held out a slim hand and he took it in his large tanned one. 'Hi, you must be Ella. I'm Lewis James, Harriet's new husband.'

'I recognised you from pictures in film magazines,' said Ella. 'It's really nice of you to ask me down. I mean, not many men would want intruders on their honeymoon.'

He smiled and stepped back to let her in, taking one of her suitcases from her as he did so. 'It's not just a honeymoon; I'm afraid I'm having to do some work as well, which means that Harriet's glad to have other people around. Some mutual friends are here too.'

'Just the same it's really nice of you,' Ella repeated, thinking that his photos, good as they were, hadn't done him justice. He was incredibly handsome and his charisma was palpable even in the few minutes they'd been speaking. Lucky Harriet, she thought to herself.

'Haven't I met you before?' asked Lewis as they

approached the dining room.

'I think I'd remember if we had,' laughed Ella.

Lewis frowned. 'I know I recognise your face. Let me think a minute. I've got it – you were in Mike Kitt's fringe production of *A Midsummer Night's Dream* weren't you? Playing Titania?'

Ella nodded. 'Yes, but I didn't think many people would have seen it.'

'I didn't see it, I saw pictures from it and a friend of mine who went said that you were incredible. The sexiest fairy queen ever according to him!'

'I had a sexy Oberon playing opposite me, that helped,' she said with a smile.

'Now we've met I wish I had seen it,' said Lewis softly, and Ella's stomach felt as though she'd just driven over a bump in the road as it lurched violently. She was still reeling from the impact Lewis had made on her as she walked into the dining room and was greeted by a delighted Harriet, who then introduced her to Edmund and Noella.

Later, helping Ella unpack in the tiny attic room at the top of the house, Harriet told her some more about the pair, explaining why it was that they were there.

'She's attractive in a rather brash way, isn't she?' mused Ella.

'Yes, I guess she is,' said Harriet. 'What did you think of Edmund?'

'Not a lot. He isn't particularly friendly is he? But your husband, Harriet, is simply gorgeous!

You must be the luckiest woman in the world.'

'I suppose so,' said Harriet.

Ella stared at her. 'You *suppose* so? Believe me, most women would kill for a husband like that.'

'I know, but he's so wrapped up in his work. It's more important to him than anything else, including our relationship.'

Ella frowned. 'Come on, Harriet, you're not complaining because he doesn't do a nine-to-five job in the local building society are you? What did you expect from one of the world's leading film directors? Anyway, when you last wrote to me you were the happiest woman alive.'

Harriet sighed. 'It's just that he seems willing to risk—'

'Risk what?'

'Nothing, I'm being stupid. You're right of course. And besides, I want a different kind of life, that's why I went to work for him in the first place.'

'Yes, and don't you forget it. Talking of that, I hear he's working on a sequel to *Dark Secret*.'

'Yes, he is. In fact, he's working on it while we're here.'

'Who's going to play Helena this time?'

'He doesn't know yet. It's giving him quite a few headaches.'

'What's the story about?' asked Ella eagerly.

'I really don't know, Ella. He doesn't discuss it with me,' said Harriet. She had intended to confide more in her friend, but there was something about Ella's enthusiasm for Lewis that

124

made her cautious. Besides, she could hardly discuss the way the film was being written with a professional actress, or the news would soon be all over London which would certainly not please Lewis.

'I'm so tired,' said Ella suddenly, lying down on her bed and closing her eyes. 'The traffic was ghastly and the car got so hot I thought I'd boil alive.'

'You have an early night,' suggested Harriet. 'The bathroom next door is just for you. Get up when you like in the morning; we see to our own breakfast. Mrs Webster's here, but Lewis prefers her to keep out of our way until he's fully conscious! She'll leave a tray of tea outside your door about eight but if you don't want to get out of bed just leave it.'

'What bliss,' sighed Ella. 'You don't know how lucky you are, Harriet.'

'Perhaps I don't,' agreed Harriet, quietly walking out of the room.

'You didn't tell me how attractive she was,' said Lewis when Harriet rejoined the others.

'You knew she was an actress.'

'Sure, but there are lots of actresses who aren't as attractive as Ella.'

'I didn't think she was particularly striking,' said Edmund. 'Rather too pale for my liking.'

'She was Titania in Mike Kitt's fringe *Dream*,' said Lewis.

'I heard that Oberon was a better fairy queen!' laughed Noella.

'According to a friend of mine Ella was excellent,' responded Lewis.

Harriet looked at him in surprise. 'My goodness, she has made a good impression on you! Well, it's mutual; she seems to imagine you're some kind of god.'

Lewis grinned. 'Good taste as well, what more can a man desire?'

'I warned you about your own desires,' Harriet whispered in his ear.

Lewis turned his head and looked thoughtfully at her. 'So you did. I'd quite forgotten that. Right, I'm off to the pub.'

'To meet Mark?' asked Harriet.

'No, just for a drink with the locals. It helps me get the atmosphere of the place. Anyone else want to join me?'

'I wouldn't mind,' said Noella. 'I've never spent a night drinking in an English pub. I hope it's a better custom than the shepherds' pie!'

'What about you, Edmund?' asked Lewis.

Edmund shook his head. 'There's no novelty for me in an English pub. Nor for Harriet either, I imagine. Shall we stay here, Harriet? We can always have a round of pitch-and-putt in the falling dusk.'

Harriet's mouth went dry and her heart started to race. 'Sure, that sounds like a good idea. I find pubs too smoky anyway.'

'As you like,' said Lewis easily. 'We'll be an hour or so I expect. Be good both of you!'

As the sound of the car engine died away,

Harriet and Edmund looked at each other and then Edmund held out his hand. 'Come along, Harriet,' he said gently. 'It's time we got to know each other a little better.'

'What about Ella?' asked Harriet, suddenly anxious to delay the moment.

'She looked ready to sleep for hours. What's the matter? Have you changed your mind?'

'No, of course not.'

He sighed with satisfaction. 'I spent a lot of time this morning arranging things in case we had an opportunity like this. I'm sure you won't be disappointed, Harriet.'

'Was that before or after you watched me in the pool?' she asked.

'Before, but it doesn't make any difference. I'm good at adapting things to meet new requirements.' Silently she took his outstretched hand and went with him.

Once inside the bedroom, Edmund sat on the side of the bed and looked up at Harriet. 'Tell me, Harriet, what is it you want of me?' he asked softly.

'I'd have thought that was obvious,' replied Harriet, her fingers moving to the front of her dress.

'Don't undo anything yet,' he said quickly. 'I want to know exactly what it is you expect of me.'

'I don't expect anything.'

'You're in love with Lewis, aren't you?' he continued as though she hadn't spoken.

'Yes, of course.'

'Then why are you here with me?'

127

Harriet took a deep breath and tried to be as honest as she could without giving away the fact that she, Edmund and his wife were part of Lewis's new film. 'I find you fascinating,' she admitted. 'There's something about you that makes me feel strange – as though through you I can learn more about myself.'

'More than Lewis can teach you?'

'Yes, because Lewis is in love with me and you're not.'

He nodded. 'That makes sense, although it's always possible that you're wrong about me.'

'In what way?'

'Never mind in what way. So, you want to learn more about yourself through me, despite the fact that in doing so you're putting your marriage at risk?'

'Lewis won't find out. How could he? Neither you nor I will tell him.'

'That's probably true as well. All right, Harriet, I accept your explanation. What I want to know now, before we carry on any further, is how far you're prepared to go?'

As soon as he'd spoken, Harriet realised that these were the words she'd hoped to hear from him, the words that she'd imagined him saying the first time they were together. He was giving her the chance to accept him totally or turn away now, and she had no doubt at all about what course of action she'd take. And that course was because of her own desires, and had nothing at all to do with Lewis's film.

'All the way,' she said clearly.

Edmund's light brown eyes lit up and a look of approval crossed his face. 'You know, Harriet, I have the feeling that you and I are going to get along very well together. Take off the dress now, we mustn't waste any more time.'

'There's just one thing,' said Harriet.

'Yes?'

'If at any time I want to stop – call the whole thing off – I can, can't I?'

'Naturally,' he said smoothly.

Harriet wasn't sure she believed him, but that sense of uncertainty, of danger, coupled with the fact that at last she was giving way to her most secret desires, made her ignore her disquiet. 'That's all right then.' She smiled as she started to unbutton her dress.

Once they were both naked, Edmund took a large jar of lubricating gel from his dressing table and dipped the fingers of his right hand in it. 'I'm going to cover your whole body with this,' he murmured. 'Don't ask why, it will all become clear later.'

Fascinated, Harriet stood still and let his hands move over her body. He worked in a detached fashion, carefully smoothing the cool gel over her upper torso, beneath her armpits, and down over her stomach. Then he turned her and did the same down her back, stopping only when he reached the cleft at the top of her buttocks.

'Bend down and touch your toes,' he said. As she bent forward his fingers smoothed the gel between the taut globes of her buttocks as well as over the gently rounded curves themselves.

Harriet began to tremble with excitement but Edmund remained very calm; and it was only when he'd spread the lubricant down the backs of her legs and turned her to face him again that she saw by his erection how aroused he was.

He then knelt in front of her and spread the lotion up the front of her legs and over her thighs. Harriet's whole body started to quiver as he smoothed it into the creases at the tops of her legs, but to her disappointment he didn't touch her between them. Finally he stepped back and studied her thoughtfully. 'That seems fine. Next the blindfold. You don't object, do you?'

Remembering the previous time, Harriet certainly didn't object and she smiled as she shook her head. Edmund didn't smile back, but by now she was accustomed to his serious approach and wasn't disappointed. In fact, if anything, his aloof disciplined approach increased her desire.

Once her eyes were covered she waited for him to ease her back on the bed, but instead she heard a door open and then there was the sound of someone else entering the room, and the mattress creaked as the newcomer lay down on it.

'Who's that?' she asked nervously.

'Relax, it isn't Lewis,' said Edmund, stroking her softly across her breasts until her nipples began to swell. 'You can lie back now,' he added, and before she could protest or even work out what was happening he was laying her down on the bed. Within seconds she was spread-eagled on another man's body, her back to his chest, and Edmund was fastening their wrists and ankles together with soft cords.

'I wish you could see yourself, Harriet,' he whispered as she squirmed against the unknown man and felt his erection starting to nudge between her well-lubricated buttocks. 'You look incredible. Part her legs for me,' he continued, but in a far harsher tone of voice, and to Harriet's surprise she felt the man's legs move beneath her, and as they spread out so did hers, leaving her totally exposed.

She realised that the man must somewhere near her own height, which meant that it certainly wasn't Lewis, but that didn't stop her from feeling horribly vulnerable tied to one man while another stood over her, free to use her as he wished.

'Arch your back and push her breasts up,' said Edmund, and she felt the well-muscled chest beneath her heave off the bed and her breasts lifted up.

Edmund's fingers swirled around the nipples and areolae, and the soft caress made Harriet sigh despite her tension. As soon as she sighed his fingers caught hold of her left nipple and pinched it, keeping it imprisoned until the ache of desire started to turn into something darker and less pleasant. Just at the moment when it started to hurt he released it, and the sense of loss startled her.

'I think you liked that more than you thought,' murmured Edmund, studying her blue veined breasts and watching them continue to swell. 'Let's try it on the other one. Push her up again, please.'

Once more the body beneath her arched and again the process was repeated, only this time the nipple was kept imprisoned for a few seconds longer so that she actually felt a flash of strange discomfort that was still pleasure – but only just – lance through her.

Sitting beside her, Edmund began to suck on each of the red and pointed nipples in turn, drawing them out to their fullest extent between his teeth before releasing them. He played with them until the excitement began to rise further down her body and she moved her hips restlessly against the unknown man.

Immediately she felt his erection increase in size until it was caught between the greased cheeks of her bottom, and when she clenched her buttocks she felt the soft velvet glans between the very top of them and he gasped at the unexpected stimulation.

'You're not expected to have a climax,' said Edmund coldly and Harriet wondered who the man was and how he could possibly control himself. 'Where would you like to be touched next, Harriet?' mused Edmund. 'Don't respond vocally, show me with your body movements.'

Harriet tried to bend her knees and part her thighs but she'd forgotten that the man she was lying on was far stronger than she was and he opposed her, so that in the end she could move nothing until he once more arched his back and pushed her breasts upwards.

'Still the breasts?' queried Edmund. 'Very well then, the breasts it is.'

'No!' said Harriet, 'I didn't move them. He did.'

'I'm afraid speaking doesn't count,' laughed Edmund and he picked up a tiny vibrator and began to run it round the circumference of each of Harriet's breasts before letting it play over her painfully hard nipples.

The fact that she was unable to see what was happening, was tied to another man and could feel his hardness at her back, combined with the delicious sensations her breasts were experiencing, was enough to give Harriet her first orgasm. Edmund watched as a tiny tremor ran right through her, causing the trapped man on the bed to groan as he struggled to control his excitement.

'Delicious!' exclaimed Edmund. 'However, I think it's time to move on. Where now?'

This time the man beneath Harriet allowed her to push upward with her belly as she forced the lower half of her torso towards Edmund. 'Support her like that,' Edmund murmured, and picking up a wide-toothed comb he drew it sideways across her abdomen, travelling from hip to hip across the lubricated flesh.

Harriet squirmed at the rippling sensations that began to fill her, and when Edmund changed direction and drew the comb down from her belly-button to the top of her pubic hair she thought that she'd go mad with excitement, her shaking body increasing the other man's pleasure as well.

'That's lovely,' cried Harriet, unable to keep silent a moment longer. 'It feels incredible, please don't stop.' Edmund didn't reply, but instead began to swirl the comb in tiny circles, lowering it down over the bottom half of her stomach until he was on the delicate area above the pubic bone.

By pressing her body down onto the solid flesh beneath her, Harriet found that she was able to intensify the sensations and she ground herself mercilessly against the stranger, her buttocks pressing against his abdomen. She heard him groan with muffled anguish as his climax threatened but she couldn't stop because Edmund wouldn't stop, and her body was lost in the wonderful feelings that were spreading through every part of her.

All at once, just as she started to feel the heat of her orgasm, Edmund lifted the comb off her body and put it to one side. Harriet cried out with disappointment but he simply put a finger to her mouth and traced the outline of her soft, supple lips. 'All in good time,' he promised her. Harriet drew the fingers into her mouth and sucked hungrily on it, like a child at the breast.

Edmund was taken aback by the power of her passion, and for a moment he considered ending all their torment and taking her there and then, but as usual his desire to prolong everything won and regretfully he removed his finger and turned his attention once more to Harriet's body.

'Open your legs,' he said brusquely to the man and her legs were spread as the other man moved his in quick obedience. 'Noella loves these,' continued Edmund, and she heard the faint buzz of the twin vibrators starting up.

Her arousal heightened and she felt as though she was melting between her thighs as her natural lubrication began to increase, until she was wetter than ever before. 'Now you see why I didn't waste the jelly there,' said Edmund in an amused voice. 'This should be enjoyable for both of you.'

All at once one of the vibrators was playing around the tops of her outspread thighs and she thrust upwards with her hips, her body parting company with that of the unknown man.

'Stay with her,' said Edmund fiercely, and she felt the man's body lift until it was once more supporting her. She was open and totally vulnerable now and Edmund felt his testicles tighten in anticipation of what was to come, but he maintained control and very gently ran the vibrator across the area between her vagina and her anus. Mentally and physically, Harriet was already balanced on the edge of her orgasm, and this gentle vibration of such highly sensitive tissue tipped her over with an abruptness that took her by surprise.

All her muscles knotted in a sharp spasm that then exploded outwards and, with a scream of delight, she felt the moment of release rush through her. Her fastened legs and arms tried to flail around the bed, but the man she was lying on had been given his instructions earlier and knew that he had to keep her as still as possible. He strained to keep her motionless and as a result her orgasm stopped just before the final tremors, leaving her still tight and aroused.

With a smile of approval for the man, Edmund promptly ran the second vibrator down beneath Harriet's body so that it touched the man's perineum, and at the same time increased the setting. For the man, who was totally unprepared, it was too much to bear. He'd already had the stimulation of Harriet's body constantly twisting and pressing against his, and his erection was trapped between her tight buttocks. Now, with this final trigger, he felt the tingling in his glans spread right down the shaft and he lost all control as the vibrator continued to play over him, while Harriet writhed and moaned in her attempts to force a totally satisfying climax from her body.

Edmund watched the man's face contort in fear and despair and then Harriet felt the warmth of his semen as it erupted from him and ran down the base of her back and across the cheeks of her bottom.

'How very ill-mannered of you,' said Edmund softly. 'I think now you should make sure that Harriet's fully satisfied. Cross your legs.'

Harriet could feel the man's body totally limp and relaxed beneath her and heard his groan of dismay at the instruction, but somehow he forced himself to obey and lifted his legs wearily across each other until Harriet's legs were crossed as well.

'Squeeze your thigh muscles in a steady rhythm,' said Edmund to Harriet.

'I want you inside me,' complained Harriet.

'Soon, but first I want to see you finish off your last climax. It ended too soon, didn't it?'

'Yes, but—'

'Then start squeezing. You'll be amazed at the result.'

Frantic for any kind of satisfaction, Harriet began to squeeze as he said and quickly felt the first flickers of an orgasm. The flickers increased in strength until they were more like tiny electric shocks that filled the whole of her pelvic area, and all at once the glorious drumming pulse began to beat behind her clitoris and she knew that in a few seconds she'd be there.

As she worked her muscles, her buttocks clenched as well and the man beneath her had to endure his now flaccid penis being re-stimulated far sooner than he would have wished, but to his amazement as he listened to Harriet's tiny cries of excitement, cries that grew louder and louder as her orgasm approached, he felt himself start to stiffen again.

Edmund watched Harriet closely. Her hair clung damply to her head and her mouth had parted showing the edges of her teeth as she gave herself over to the pure unadulterated luxury of the entire experience. 'Now, Harriet,' he said quickly. 'Clench harder. I want you to come *now*.'

'Yes!' screamed Harriet, as his words provided the final stimulus that enabled her to climax yet again, and this time her legs and arms moved wildly because the exhausted man below her lacked the strength to restrain her.

'Excellent,' said Edmund. 'Perhaps it's time for me to take my turn.'

He waited a few moments for Harriet's body to recover and then lay down on top of her. She found herself trapped between the two men, and the sensation was so new and thrilling that she felt her body begin to swell at the mere thought of what was happening to her.

Edmund moved his body up and down over hers. He rubbed his nipples against her breasts, swirled his tongue in her ear and rotated his lower body hard against hers, slipping one leg between her thighs and then ordering the other man to bring his legs together so that Harriet's clitoris was stimulated by it.

She was utterly lost. Her body was nothing but a mass of incredible sensations and her excitement had driven away all sense of fear or shame. This was what she wanted from Edmund, this was what she'd sensed he could show her, and she was revelling in every minute of it.

Gently Edmund slid his rigid erection up her inner channel and then positioned his legs outside those of the other man which meant that Harriet's legs were closed tightly around his shaft and her clitoral stimulation was greater.

He knew that he wouldn't last very long, that the preliminaries had taken all his self-control, but he didn't care because he also knew that after this Harriet would return for more. He moved quickly but rhythmically inside her, and she clenched the walls of her vagina tightly about him, determined to force him into a speedy orgasm because that was what she wanted.

Edmund didn't resist. He allowed her to milk him, to draw his seed upwards and just as he came he shouted for the other man to lift his hips and this slight alteration of angle meant that Harriet came at the same time, almost sobbing with the intensity of the moment.

At last Edmund collapsed on top of her, ignoring the man trapped beneath them both. 'You were magnificent,' he murmured, and behind her blindfold Harriet basked in his admiration.

When he'd recovered, Edmund got up and carefully untied Harriet's wrists and ankles before pulling her to her feet, allowing the man to slip out of the room before he finally removed her blindfold. She looked around, seeking some clue as to his identity.

'You know who it was, really,' said Edmund.

She recalled the firmly muscled body of the man, his height and the easy way in which he'd restrained her. 'Yes, I suppose I do, but I'd rather it was kept a secret.'

'Of course,' agreed Edmund. 'There are many

things that are better left to the imagination. What will you tell Lewis you were doing while he was at the pub?' he added casually.

Harriet smiled. 'I'm not sure, and right at this moment I'm not too bothered. He's the one who keeps leaving us alone together.'

'I don't want him told,' said Edmund sharply.

Harriet, who knew that Lewis would learn every detail either from herself or from some camera that she was certain he had concealed in the room, looked at him questioningly. 'Why not?'

'Because he isn't the kind of man you should make a fool of.'

'I don't suppose many men are,' murmured Harriet.

'Just the same, be careful,' said Edmund. 'I've got a lot of money riding on your husband. The last thing I want to do is upset the status quo at this point in time.'

Harriet wanted to laugh when she thought about what Edmund would think if he knew that he was the one being used, and that Lewis had counted on him to seduce her in order to be able to script the very film that Edmund wanted to make him money, but she didn't think that Edmund would appreciate the joke.

Pulling her dress over her still tingling flesh, she turned to leave the room and was surprised when Edmund caught hold of her arm. 'Aren't you going to kiss me before you go?' he asked softly.

'No,' replied Harriet.

'Why not?'

'A kiss is a gesture of affection, or even love. That isn't what this is all about.'

He nodded. 'How wise you are, Harriet. It's strange, but I thought women had to be emotionally involved before they could lose all their inhibitions in the way you did just now.'

'Did you?' asked Harriet. 'Then it seems that you don't know everything.' But as she made her way to her own room in order to bath and change she wondered if he was right. She hoped not, because if she became emotionally involved with Edmund it would lead to nothing but disaster for them all.

In the crowded Cornish pub Lewis sat drinking a pint of real ale and jotted down notes on a small pad while Noella watched him thoughtfully. 'It's all grist to your mill, Lewis, isn't it?' she laughed at last. 'Even a quiet drink in a pub is an opportunity to study people.'

'I won't be coming back to Cornwall. I have to get the people right,' he retorted.

'Has marrying Harriet stopped you fancying other women?' she murmured as a tall leggy blonde walked by their table and smiled warmly at him.

'Hardly. It just stops me doing anything about it.'

'You mean you're intending to be faithful?'

With a sigh Lewis put down his pad. 'All right, you've got my attention. What are you trying to say?'

'Only this, honey: your lovely young bride isn't the kind of lady who should be neglected. She may not have such good self-control as you, since she doesn't have any job to consume her passion when sex is lacking.'

'Sex isn't lacking from our marriage!' laughed Lewis.

'But you leave her alone a lot,' Noella pointed out.

'She isn't alone. Edmund is there with her.'

'And you trust Edmund?' asked Noella in astonishment.

Lewis leant back in his chair and looked at her through narrowed eyes. 'Don't you?'

'Not one bit, and certainly not with a beautiful sexy girl like Harriet.'

'Then why are you here with me? You could have stayed at Penruan and acted as chaperone.'

'I'd made other plans but they were cancelled at the last moment and I didn't fancy an evening in.'

'Did these other plans include Oliver Kesby by any chance?'

Noella nodded. 'They did. We had a great time last night, and were all booked up for tonight when he stood me up. He said he'd forgotten he'd promised to see some friends, but I don't believe him.'

'Why not? He seems very smitten. I don't think he'd pass up the chance of some time alone with you if he could help it,' said Lewis.

'Are you taken with me, Lew?' murmured

142

Noella, reaching out across the table and running her fingers round the inside of his hand which was resting palm uppermost on the table.

'You're a very exciting and sexy woman,' said Lewis carefully.

Noella gave a short laugh. 'In other words, you don't fancy me.'

'Perhaps I've known you too long. We're friends, you know that, but there's no sexual chemistry there, at least not for me.'

Noella had known what the answer would be but she was still disappointed. 'How about Harriet's friend? Do you fancy her?'

'I'm busy with a film script and I'm also on my honeymoon! I haven't given Ella more than a fleeting glance.'

Noella leant forward, her elbows on the table. 'This film, Lewis. What's it about?'

'Forbidden desires.'

She shivered with mock excitement. 'How intriguing. What kind of forbidden desires?'

'The kind that cause disasters,' said Lewis slowly. 'The kind that lead people to do thoroughly reckless things, things they may regret for the rest of their lives, simply because the lure of the forbidden is more than they can resist.'

'You're talking about sex I take it?' queried Noella.

Lewis let out a soft sigh. 'I was when I first began the film, but now I'm realising that it can be other things too. Take me for instance. You rightly point out that I could be risking my marriage to the one woman who I know can make me happy in order to get on with a film that's proving more and more alluring with every day that passes. I don't suppose that's too different from a forbidden sexual thrill.'

'Does it all end happily?' enquired Noella.

'I've no idea.'

'You should put Oliver and me in it,' said Noella innocently. 'He's just the sort of man I know I should stay away from. He's too young for me, and too poor, but he offers the kind of sex I like best and don't get any more. Wouldn't you say that's a risky combination?'

'Yes, I would. So, what makes you let it happen?'

She grinned. 'Like you say, the fact that I know I shouldn't!'

'Surely you and Edmund are happy?' probed Lewis, and Noella was surprised at how worried he looked.

'We used to be, but it's not the same these days. I'm getting tired of being what Edmund wants rather than what I want. I guess I've spent too long pretending to be something I'm not. Basically I'm a simple girl from a simple background.'

'With expensive tastes!' Lewis pointed out.

'Yeah, unfortunately with expensive tastes. But it's not just one-way; Edmund is getting tired of me. He knows my heart isn't in it these days and that's kind of irritating for him.'

'You mean he's tired of the marriage too?' asked Lewis in genuine dismay.

'I sure as hell don't see us lasting another ten years,' said Noella, without any apparent distress. 'We've had a good time but we've grown apart. He needs someone different. Someone more like Harriet, I'd say.'

The colour drained from Lewis's face, but he tried to make light of her remark. 'There aren't many girls like Harriet around.'

'Then maybe you should concentrate on hanging on to the one you've got.'

Lewis shook his head. 'You don't understand, Noella. I have to be able to trust her.'

'She's very much in love with you,' said Noella. 'What's the point in deliberately putting temptation in her path? It isn't fair to either of you.'

'I can't turn back now,' muttered Lewis. 'There's too much riding on it.'

'Well, have it your own way, but I think you're a fool. Say, isn't that your friend Mark coming in the door?'

Lewis glanced up. 'Great. I hoped he might turn up. Look, Noella, as he is here I really should talk business with him. Will you be all right if I get you another drink and join him at the bar, or would you rather go back to Penruan?'

'I'll go back to Penruan,' said Noella, making no attempt to hide her feelings of surprise. 'But I must say, Lewis, that you've got a great deal more selfish in the past few months.'

'Well, that's what happens when people are

depending on you to make them a lot of money, like your husband,' said Lewis.

'She looked ticked off,' commented Mark as the two of them sat down by the bar. 'Edmund not keeping her happy?'

'It seems not,' said Lewis. 'I just hope he isn't keeping anyone else too happy either. Get your pen out, we've a lot to discuss.'

Chapter Seven

WHEN NOELLA ARRIVED back at Penruan after her evening at the pub with Lewis, she was surprised to encounter Oliver leaving the house, and he looked both surprised and embarrassed to see her.

'I hope you and your friends had a good evening,' she said sarcastically as her mind raced, trying to work out what he could have been doing in the house.

'It was all right,' he murmured, trying to slip past her, but Noella refused to let him off so lightly.

'Is there something wrong in the house?' she enquired.

'Wrong?'

'I thought you must be doing some kind of late night service.' Noella had a distinct edge to her voice.

Oliver, who thought Noella was the sexiest

woman he'd ever made love to, wished that he could tell her the truth: that Edmund had told him he knew of the younger man's affair with his wife but would turn a blind eye to it providing he helped him this evening. 'There was an air-lock in the water system,' he said quickly.

'Who called you out?'

'Your husband. Noella, can we meet up tomorrow evening instead? I'd really like to see you again.'

'I'll let you know,' said Noella shortly, her pride already bruised by Lewis's behaviour earlier.

Oliver suddenly reached out and pulled her towards him, his mouth covering hers in a fiercely urgent kiss as his hands pinioned the sides of her arms. 'I really want you,' he whispered.

Noella pulled herself free and then let one of her hands travel down the front of his jeans. Despite his experience earlier that night, Oliver was relieved to find that he was hard again and he watched Noella's expression with pride. 'I can tell that you do,' she conceded, smiling at last. 'I'll try and arrange something. How would you feel about a threesome?' she added thoughtfully.

Oliver swallowed. He didn't think he could tell her that he'd just taken part in one – albeit in a minor role – and found it incredibly arousing. 'It depends on the sex of the third person,' he said slowly. 'I'd enjoy two women, but not another man.'

'It was a woman I had in mind,' Noella assured

him, thinking of Ella. 'It's something that always turns me on. I'll work on it.'

'Fine,' agreed Oliver, his head spinning. On the way back to his cottage he thanked his good fortune in having Lewis and his entourage choose Penruan for their six week stay in England.

Later that night Noella climbed into bed and joined Edmund, who was lying on his back staring at the ceiling. 'I take it you had an enjoyable evening?' she asked.

'Excellent thank you. Was Lewis good company?'

'No, he was not! I don't understand that man. I tried to warn him about the dangers of neglecting Harriet but I don't think he listened. He was more interested in his next film.'

'You did what?' asked Edmund, sitting upright and glaring at her.

'Warned him about leaving Harriet alone so much.'

'I've never interfered in your extra-marital activities and I don't expect you to start interfering in mine now,' said Edmund coldly.

'Why not? My affairs have never threatened our marriage – Harriet does.'

'And that worries you?' he asked sardonically.

'Of course it does,' said Noella fiercely. 'I told Lewis it didn't, that our marriage was virtually over, but that was only to try and prod him into some kind of action. I need you, Edmund, you know that.'

'I don't know any such thing. You need my

149

money, but in the event of a divorce I'd be more than generous, I promise you.'

Noella clutched at his arm. 'Harriet is special to you, isn't she?'

'She's certainly different,' he conceded.

'But she's in love with Lewis.'

'Then that makes it all the more of a challenge.'

'A forbidden desire?' asked Noella quietly.

Edmund looked surprised. 'How very perceptive of you. Yes, a forbidden desire.'

'Doesn't that make you suspicious?' asked Noella.

'I don't know what you mean.'

'It's the title of Lewis's next film.'

'So what?'

Noella hadn't clawed her way up from poverty to wealth without having more than her fair share of shrewd intelligence. 'You don't think he might be using you?'

'By handing me Harriet on a plate? I think that's highly unlikely. You know as well as I do that he's besotted with her. Only an idiot would deliberately take the risk of losing someone who was that precious to him. No, Lewis is just being Lewis and going his own sweet way without noticing the effect he's having on those around him.'

'But what if he *is* using you? How would you feel about your precious Harriet then?'

Edmund shook his head in disbelief. 'You're saying that Harriet's in on this too? That she's helping him with the plot by having an affair?'

'It's possible.'

150

'No,' Edmund assured her. 'After what happened here tonight I have to contradict you. It isn't possible. Harriet is doing what she wants to do. No one dictates to Harriet, she's surprisingly independent.'

'What did go on here tonight?' queried Noella.

Edmund yawned. 'I forget the details but it was all very exhausting. Time to sleep I think.'

'Did you have trouble with the hot water?' asked Noella as Edmund was dropping off to sleep.

'No. Why?'

'I was curious that's all. It made a few strange noises when I ran my bath and I wondered if it was faulty.'

'It wasn't earlier on. If it's still playing up in the morning let Oliver know.'

'Believe me, I will,' said Noella. Long after Edmund was asleep she lay awake pondering on her future and also on what Oliver had really been doing in the house that night.

In the next bedroom Harriet was fast asleep when Lewis at last returned from the pub but he woke her just the same. She mumbled sleepily as she tried to roll away from him.

'Tell me about it,' said Lewis, his voice low and urgent. 'I have to know all the details before I see Mark again tomorrow.'

Harriet struggled to wake up. 'I don't want to talk about it,' she complained.

'But you have to! That's the whole point of the affair. Are you enjoying it? Do you feel at all guilty or does the pleasure blot that out of your mind? Harriet, wake up and talk to me.'

Harriet rubbed at her eyes like a child and Lewis felt a rush of tenderness for her. What he really wanted to do was take her in his arms and make slow gentle love to her until she climaxed with that sweet intensity that he found so moving.

'I'm sorry, Harriet, but you know we've got to do this. Besides, if we don't talk about it the whole thing becomes more dangerous.'

Harriet moved extra pillows behind her back and propped herself up a little. 'More dangerous, Lew? I honestly don't see how that's possible. Once you gave me the freedom to follow my desires the dangers were obvious. You can't talk them away.'

'It's a film, for God's sake, not real life!' he hissed, anxious not to disturb Edmund and Noella.

Harriet stared at him. 'That's where you're wrong, Lewis. It's a film to you, but not to me and not to Edmund either, come to that. I'm not Rowena, you know.'

'What's that supposed to mean?'

'She was a professional actress. When you set up the scenario for *Dark Secret* she knew how to act out the role you'd assigned to her, but I'm not an actress and I never have been. I was a PA, remember? When I'm with Edmund, when we're making love together, I'm not acting, I'm really doing it. That's what I was trying to tell you!

That's why this whole idea is so dangerous. Can't you tell the difference between acting and real life? Or do you believe that we're all actors at heart?'

'I suppose I do,' admitted Lewis. 'Most people are acting a great deal of the time. They're putting on the mask of a professional businessman or a hooker, but that's not the real person. The only difference between you and Rowena is that she'd had training and had a technique to fall back on when she couldn't find the real emotions.'

'Yes, well as I don't have that technique everything I feel and do comes from the heart, which is much more dangerous. Sometimes I can't believe I'm letting you do this to us,' she added.

'Then tell me you want to stop,' said Lewis quietly. 'If you ask me to drop the project and find another idea, then I will.'

Harriet stared at him in astonishment. Her body was already remembering the sensations it had experienced at Edmund's hands, and the incredible excitement of finding itself trapped between two men, both of whom were revelling in her abandoned sexuality.

'Give it all up?' she asked slowly.

'Yes, if that's what you want then tell me.' He was watching her very closely as he spoke and saw the conflict in her eyes.

'I can't,' she admitted, her voice so quiet he had to strain to hear the words. 'It's too late for that now. I have to see it through to the end.'

153

Lewis nodded. 'So he's as exciting as you'd imagined?'

'Yes.'

'But you still want to blame me for your forbidden pleasure?'

'I can't blame you,' she admitted, 'but I do know that I'd never have started the affair if you hadn't said I could.'

'It wasn't exactly like that,' he said gently. 'Harriet, do you love him?'

'No. He isn't the kind of man I'd ever love.'

'Then there's nothing to worry about. Now, tell me what you did.'

They were all late down to breakfast the next morning, but for the first time, Edmund joined them, and Lewis couldn't help noticing the way the other man studied Harriet as she moved around the table, pouring freshly squeezed orange juice into glasses. Her legs were bare beneath her lemon-coloured shorts with ivory stripes, and she wore a matching waistcoat over a scoop-neck short-sleeved white ribbed top. Already her skin was starting to glow with the change of air and her face had a faint tinge of natural colour that accentuated her high cheekbones and the alertness of her grey eyes. Any normal red-blooded male would admire her, conceded Lewis, but he didn't care for the almost proprietary interest that Edmund seemed to take.

'I trust you slept well, Harriet,' had been Edmund's only words to her, but even that had irritated Lewis. It was too English, and seemed calculated to make him feel like an outsider rather than Harriet's husband.

He realised that he was being paranoid. The few details that he'd managed to extract from Harriet about her evening's activities hadn't been the sort to set him at ease, and he'd known that she was keeping a lot back. In order to find out the rest he had to retrieve the film from the concealed camera in Edmund's room some time that day, but he wasn't sure he really wanted to see it.

'Are we going to Morwellham Quay this morning?' asked Noella, draining her fruit juice and reaching for an apple. 'If we are I must take my camera. Oliver says it's just great for tourists.'

'At least you won't be mistaken for anyone from the past,' remarked Edmund, glancing at his wife's vivid red skirt with split sides and her cotton T-shirt which was white but covered by masses of hand-painted pineapples, peaches and grapes. 'I think it must have been easy to be turned on by the long skirts and laced tops of olden times,' he continued. 'There's certainly something to be said for keeping your charms concealed. It adds a little frisson of excitement when you have to work hard at getting what you want.'

Harriet glanced at him from beneath lowered lids but didn't answer. Before Lewis could make any remark, Ella came into the room. She looked as though her night's sleep had refreshed her and her blue eyes were lively and full of excitement. 'What a lovely morning!' she exclaimed. Lewis was struck by her voice which was deep and obviously well trained. 'Have you any plans?' she added, looking round the room.

'Love the leggings and top, honey,' said Noella, her eyes flicking over Ella's outfit which was covered in huge sunflowers. 'Good job you're small-boned, though. I'd look too large in it.'

'No one could accuse Ella of looking too large,' said Lewis with a smile. Ella smiled back at him. She was still astonished at his sexual magnetism and wished that he hadn't just got married. She'd have given anything for a chance to spend a night or two with him, quite apart from giving her soul for a chance to work with him.

'There's this village called Morwellham Quay on the Devon border where everyone's dressed up in historic costume and works in the old-fashioned way,' explained Harriet. 'We're meant to be going there.'

'I've got Mark coming round this morning,' said Lewis awkwardly. 'Could the trip wait until after lunch?' Harriet's mouth tightened but she kept silent.

'Not really,' said Edmund, the corners of his mouth turning up slightly at the prospect of an outing without Lewis. 'Oliver said that midday is the best time to be there. You even get an old-fashioned lunch.'

'Then I'll have to forego it and have a modern one,' said Lewis shortly. He looked at Harriet.

'I'm really sorry, sweetheart. I'll make it up to you I promise, but we're at a crucial point and until we've straightened out one or two things Mark can't proceed.'

Harriet shrugged. 'That's all right. I'm sure I'll manage to enjoy myself without you.'

Ella looked sharply at her friend and saw the dark circles beneath her eyes. She wondered if they were caused by too many exhausting nights of passion or the tensions that Harriet had hinted at the previous night. 'I've been before,' she announced. 'I spent a month in Devon two years ago and remember it very well because I took masses of photos. I'm not sure I want to go again.'

'Well that's nice, Lewis will have some company,' said Noella, looking thoughtfully at Ella.

'I tell you what, why don't we invite Oliver to come along as our guide?' said Edmund suddenly. 'Three's always an awkward number and I'm sure he'd enjoy a day out for a change.'

'I'll go ask him,' said Noella quickly. 'Just make sure the water doesn't play up while he's out, Lewis.'

'Why should it?' asked Lewis, irritated by the fact that Ella would be remaining behind when he wanted to use the spare time he had to retrieve the film from Edmund's room.

'He was here late last night doing something to it, although there's a little bit of confusion over exactly who asked him over. Isn't that right, Edmund?'

Harriet felt the nape of her neck go warm and hoped she wasn't blushing. 'I'll go and collect some things,' she murmured.

'You don't mind if Oliver comes, do you Harriet?' asked Edmund quietly.

She paused at his elbow. 'Of course not.'

'I think he's earned some kind of reward.'

Remembering the way the unseen man had climaxed between her clenched buttocks the previous night, Harriet felt that if that man was – as she suspected – Oliver, then he'd already been rewarded but she could hardly say as much in front of Lewis. 'He's always working very hard,' she agreed. Edmund smiled.

An hour later the four of them had set off, Ella had gone outside to explore the grounds and Lewis and Mark were sat in the conservatory, where Lewis had made love to Harriet, discussing the film.

'What bothers me,' said Mark, 'is the way Helena's husband's behaving during her affair.'

'Bothers you?'

'I don't think he'd talk it over calmly, or even let the affair carry on once it had begun. Sure I can see how it could come about, but if this guy's as much in love with her as we've been led to believe then he'd back out.'

'It's a test,' Lewis reminded the scriptwriter. 'No doubt the husband will find it hard, and I think you should stress that, but he has to know how far Helena will go before she brings it to an end herself.'

158

'And the other guy, the lover, he's going to start falling in love with her, isn't he? Because frankly, Lew, most men watching the film will and it's hard to imagine a guy who's having such incredible sex with her not getting emotionally involved.'

'Some men don't,' pointed out Lewis.

'So he definitely won't? I don't want to find myself rewriting this from a different angle later on when you change your mind.'

'I think,' said Lewis carefully, 'that you'd better leave it slightly open. Allow for the possibility that he might get more involved than anyone expects.'

'There isn't going to be a murder at the end of this is there? Only murder isn't my scene.'

Lewis smiled. 'No, there won't be a murder. A kind of death perhaps, the death of love or trust, but not a murder.'

Mark frowned and leant towards his employer. 'Be careful, Lew. I don't want anyone getting hurt in this, least of all you.'

'Me? I'm just the director!'

'I think I know you too well to take that remark at face value. All I'm saying is that I'm really fond of both you and Harriet and I don't want to see you screwing up your lives for the sake of a film.'

'Thanks for the concern,' said Lewis coldly. 'However, I pay you to write, not to lecture, all right?' With a sigh, Mark started to write.

It was gone midday by the time Mark left, and nearly one o'clock before Lewis decided that he'd have a swim before going to the local pub for a snack lunch. He was beginning to think that pubs were a good idea and that perhaps the Americans should try transporting a few across the Atlantic.

Ella, lying face down on the grass with her chin in her hands, watched him pad to the poolside in his brief trunks and admired his olive-coloured skin, inherited from his Portuguese mother, as well as his muscular body and striking height which came from his Texan father. He was perfect, she thought to herself, and somehow Harriet – quiet, conventional Harriet – had managed, if the tabloids were to be believed, to tame him. Being an actress though, she knew full well that the tabloids were often wrong.

After Lewis had done ten energetic lengths he looked up to see Ella sitting at the edge of the pool, her arms wrapped round her knees. 'You're a good swimmer,' she said admiringly.

'Powerful but not stylish I'm afraid. I hope you haven't been too bored sitting out here alone. My work has a nasty habit of taking over my life, as Harriet's discovering to her cost.'

'I like being alone,' said Ella, which wasn't true but seemed the kind of answer he'd appreciate.

'That's good; far too many women seem to need constant entertainment.'

'So do some men,' retorted Ella.

He came over to her side of the pool and looked up at her, brushing his damp black hair back from his eyes. 'That's very true. I didn't mean to sound sexist.'

'It doesn't worry me,' laughed Ella. 'I enjoy the differences between men and women.'

He recognised the double meaning of the words and smiled, enjoying the game. 'So do I. Are you going to join me in the water?'

'I can't swim.'

'For lunch then? We could go to the pub down the road.'

Ella got to her feet. 'I'll ask Mrs Webster to make us up a salad and then we can have it out here without going to all the bother of getting changed for the pub.'

'Good idea,' agreed Lewis. 'I should have finished my forty lengths by the time the meal's ready.'

He was right. When Ella returned he was sitting on one of the loungers with his long legs spread out in front of him, still wearing his damp swimming trunks which did little to conceal his impressive manhood.

'How's the new film coming along?' asked Ella, handing him a tray of food and a glass of wine.

'As well as I could have hoped. The early stages are always a nightmare.'

'Tell me,' said Ella slipping off her leggings and then squatting cross-legged at the side of his chair in just her bikini bottom and T-shirt, 'who's going to play Helena this time?'

Lewis looked thoughtfully at her. 'I take it you've heard I'm looking for a new Helena?'

'Of course. Every young actress in the country has heard.'

'Well, I'm still looking,' he said enigmatically.

'Are you going to hold auditions while you're over here?'

Lewis shook his head. 'I hate auditioning people. I'll probably see the person I want on TV or at the cinema.'

'Or here, in Cornwall,' said Ella softly.

Lewis felt the hairs on the backs of his arms rise and he looked down into the depths of her blue eyes. 'Or here,' he conceded slowly.

Ella's heart was pounding as she worked out what she should do next. He was interested in her, she knew that, but she also knew that if she made the wrong move or seemed too pushy then he'd have no compunction in throwing her out of the house, even if she was Harriet's guest. Very slowly she peeled off her T-shirt, and beneath it she was naked. 'I've always thought that I had the right figure to play Helena,' she said calmly.

Lewis felt his penis stir. She was certainly very sexy, and she had the same kind of intelligence about her that had attracted him to Harriet, plus an actress's ability to convey emotions on command. Right now she was playing at seducing him, and it was working, as his body was only too eager to demonstrate.

'Helena's really Harriet, isn't she?' whispered Ella, moving her body until her legs were resting against the side of the lounger.

'What makes you say that?'

'I saw *Dark Secret* and I've known Harriet for

years. You changed one or two things, but not many.'

'I based her on Harriet,' he admitted.

'And would you need to desire the actress who played her, just as you desire Harriet?' she murmured.

Lewis looked up at Ella and felt a surge of pure lust. She was a bright, sexy and attractive girl who could easily be made beautiful for the screen. She was also flatteringly anxious to please him, although he had no illusions as to why this was, and right at this moment he was a man who felt in need of pleasure.

After Mark left he'd recovered the film from Edmund's room and watched it on his television. The searing sexuality of the scene that had unfolded before him was still printed on his brain, and he needed a woman – preferably a woman who bore some resemblance to Harriet.

'Yes, I probably would need to desire the actress,' he said in a level tone.

'I'd like to play Helena in the film,' said Ella. 'And I'd enjoy an audition. Even if you don't normally like them I think you might like this one.'

'Is that a fact?' he mused, a flicker of amusement dancing in his dark eyes.

'They won't be back for a long time,' continued Ella, deciding to gamble everything on this one moment.

'I thought you were getting over a broken heart,' Lewis reminded her.

'Work always takes my mind off things.'

'It takes my mind off food,' remarked Lewis.

To Ella's surprise he put his tray down, stood up and reached for her hand. 'Come on then, Ella. I'll audition you out here, in the shade of those bushes.'

'Out here?' Ella had been imagining a comfortable session on a soft bed.

His mouth curled. 'What's the matter? Isn't your acting ability up to it?'

Ella's stomach tightened with desire. 'Of course. I wasn't sure that we'd have privacy, that was all.'

'Surely actresses are used to an audience,' he teased as they moved into the shade. 'But I know what you mean, and we'll have total privacy I promise you.'

Ella glanced around her. As far as she could see there was no one in sight, and anyway she realised that she had to go along with anything that Lewis said if she wanted to get the part, and she did. She wanted the part almost as much as she wanted an affair with Lewis James.

Once they were out of the sun, Lewis sat down on the ground in front of Ella and his strong hands tugged at the sides of her blue bikini bottom until he'd lowered it to just below her pubic mound. Then he let it go so that her legs were kept close together by the garment, but not so close that his tongue couldn't touch her where she most wanted to feel it.

Lewis, though, chose to begin higher up. He

164

positioned her feet in between his knees and then licked very lightly at the flesh that covered her hip bones, while at the same time his nose nudged against the muscles that were jumping wildly to the side of her hips. Ella tried to move, to get him to travel lower, but he refused to be hurried and she had to content herself with reaching down and clasping her left hand round the back of his head.

Ella's bikini line had been waxed and she'd also removed most of her hair that normally covered the top of her pubic mound, leaving just a narrow strip leading up from the top join of the outer lips. This meant that when Lewis travelled lower he could tongue freely against the enticingly soft skin of this delicate area and he found it extraordinarily arousing.

He tried to imagine Harriet's body similarly bare and at once his tongue moved more urgently until at last, to Ella's delight, he was parting her outer sex lips and allowing his tongue to travel slowly down between the inner lips until he reached the tiny clitoris that was slowly becoming erect.

When he eased back the protective hood with his nose and then drew the small button between his lips, Ella's legs started to shake and her free hand went to her right breast, the fingers kneading at the expanding tissue so that she was being stimulated in both the areas she liked best.

Looking down at Lewis's head of blue-black hair working enthusiastically between her thighs

Ella could scarcely believe what was happening to her, and without warning a swift climax shook her body causing her to gasp aloud at the unexpected pleasure.

Lewis waited for the tremors to die away and then licked the middle finger of his left hand before moving it round between her taut buttocks. Ella bent her knees to accommodate him and he softly drew his fingertip in circles around the outside of her anus while his tongue continued to flick and caress her clitoral area.

Intense flashes of the most incredible pleasure ran from the back to the front of Ella's body and she felt her abdominal muscles tighten as a fierce tension began to build within her. Lewis knew that now she was approaching a large orgasm and his own excitement mounted. In his mind she wasn't Ella, she was Harriet, and when she whimpered and pleaded with him to carry on it was Harriet's voice that he heard.

Ella bent her legs a little further and at this invitation Lewis allowed his finger to slip inside her back passage where he softly stroked the inside rim, pressing delicately on the highly sensitive nerve endings until Ella began to scream with excitement. Her clitoris retracted and realising that her climax was very close, Lewis drew the bikini pants right down to the ground and helped the trembling Ella to step out of them.

She was disappointed to lose the touch of his finger in such a private place and desolate at the loss of his clever tongue between her thighs; but

166

she knew that whatever followed would be even better and when he laid her on her back on the grass she spread her legs wide and stared up at him, waiting to see what he wanted of her.

Lewis knelt across her right leg and lifted her left leg high in the air so that her foot was resting on his shoulder. 'I'm going to enter you now,' he murmured. 'When I do, I want you to slide a finger in alongside me, and that way you'll stimulate me manually while I'm inside you.'

Ella had never done that before but she could hardly wait to try, and as soon as he slid his large erection inside her she reached down to obey. Because of his size it proved difficult at first and he had to withdraw a little in order for her to accomplish it. Then, with her finger lying by the side of his penis, he began to thrust. He thrust slowly and fiercely, building to a steady climax as Ella squirmed and gasped beneath him.

Ella felt her finger rubbing against his shaft and with each vigorous movement she also stimulated the ridge at the base of his glans. When this happened his breath snagged and he uttered a tiny groan on the backward movement.

She'd never felt so excited before. The fact that it was Lewis James making love to her, and that he was doing it in the open air where anyone might see them, would have been sufficient to arouse her without his incredible skill. The combination of both was almost too much for her and her orgasm built far more quickly than she wanted, making it impossible for her to prolong the moment.

'I'm coming!' she shouted and Lewis felt her internal muscles squeezing tightly around him as she yelled with wild abandon and her body bucked and thrashed on the grass.

By the time she'd finished Lewis was nearly there as well. He continued to thrust inside her, but faster now, thinking only of his own pleasure. Suddenly he had a mental image of the way Harriet had looked when she'd come beneath Edmund's knowing hands and immediately Lewis came as well, throwing back his head with a shout that was more of pain than ecstasy.

Ella's body was still twitching spasmodically and Lewis lay down on the grass next to her, their shoulders touching as both of them slowly recovered.

'You were fantastic,' said Ella, her voice husky with emotion.

'You too,' murmured Lewis, but he knew already he felt strangely empty and wanted nothing more than for Ella to go back into the house. It wasn't her fault, she'd done nothing wrong and the sex had been good, but she wasn't Harriet and emotionally he felt bereft.

Ella rolled over and lay on top of him, her breasts brushing his chest. 'Could I play her?' she asked breathlessly.

Lewis frowned. 'What?'

'Could I play Helena in the film? Was my audition satisfactory?'

'*You* were very satisfactory,' he assured her.

'I understand how much your work means to

you,' Ella assured him. 'Don't worry, I won't say a word to Harriet. After all, this was just research, wasn't it?'

'I don't know what it was,' admitted Lewis. 'You're a very desirable woman, Ella, and I'm most definitely not a saint.'

'I wouldn't want a saint. You know, you should have married an actress,' she added, rolling off him again and reaching for her clothes.

'Why?'

'Harriet's not happy because she doesn't understand you the way someone from the profession would.'

Lewis looked at her thoughtfully. 'Harriet understands me very well. I was married to Rowena Farmer before Harriet and she didn't understand me at all.'

Ella smiled. 'My mistake then. When will I know?'

'Know what?'

'If the part's mine.'

Lewis felt a flash of annoyance. 'Look, this was something we both enjoyed wasn't it? I told you, I've no idea who'll play Helena.'

'You asked me to do an outdoor audition.'

'Yes, but we both understood what I meant.'

'I hope Harriet understands that too, if I don't get the part,' said Ella sweetly as she walked away from him.

She felt guilty about it when she got back into the house. After all, she'd known he and Harriet were only just married, and knew too that she'd have slept with him whether or not there was any chance of the film part. However, now that she knew what he was like, now that she'd experienced his lovemaking for herself, she wanted to stay near him. If that was possible by appearing in his film then she'd be happy, but if not she was willing to try and take him away from Harriet. In Ella's opinion friendship ended at the bedroom door.

Lewis pulled on his swimming trunks and got wearily to his feet. For the first time in his life the transient thrill of sex hadn't been enough for him. Ella was sexy and attractive but she wasn't Harriet, and it was Harriet he wanted.

'Perhaps you were right, Mark,' he murmured to himself. 'But it's all out of my hands now.'

Luckily he didn't realise how greatly his sense of emptiness contrasted with Ella's sense of elation.

Chapter Eight

STANDING IN THE middle of his hotel room, receiver held to his ear, Mark could scarcely believe what he was hearing. 'Change the character?' he exclaimed in horror. 'I can't, not at this stage.'

'You have to,' said Lewis shortly, and Mark could hear the tension in his employer's voice over the line.

'But it won't make sense.'

'Then you must make it seem logical. After all, you were the one who kept warning me about the dangers of all this.'

'Helena's husband's character has been constant throughout both films,' said Mark patiently. 'I don't think the audience will accept a radical change at this point.'

'Contrary to what we're led to believe, people do change,' said Lewis bitterly. 'I wouldn't have believed it myself a few hours ago but now I know it's true.'

'Are you all right?' asked Mark anxiously.

'No, I'm not, but that's not important. What's important is that this film reflects the truth, and the truth is that by the time the confident, strong, emotionally-detached husband is half-way through his little experiment he discovers that he stands to lose more than he'd ever realised.'

'I tried to tell you that at the beginning,' Mark pointed out.

'Save it, Mark. Just write it the way I tell you. Our hero, if that's the right word for him, has casual but exhilarating sex with his wife's best friend and instead of thoroughly enjoying it he ends up feeling empty and annoyed.'

'With the friend?'

'No, with himself! Are you deliberately trying to wind me up?' demanded Lewis angrily.

'Only getting the facts straight. Right, so it's a sudden change but brought about by a particular incident. That makes it a bit easier for me.'

'I'm so pleased,' said Lewis sarcastically.

'So you should be; I've got to make this thing hang together. How about Helena? Is she finding her affair empty and unsatisfying too?'

'No!' retorted Lewis shortly, and Mark heard the sound of the receiver being slammed down at Penruan House.

The scriptwriter got out his notebook and began to write. It wasn't really as hard as he'd made out – he'd guessed what would happen from the very beginning.

'We had a wonderful time,' exclaimed Harriet, running into the drawing room and kissing Lewis enthusiastically. 'Wait until you see my picture.'

'Picture?'

'I had one done of me in Victorian costume, I look really demure.'

'Noella had one done too,' said Edmund, 'but she looks like someone who was on the game, don't you honey?'

Noella pulled a face. 'That's because I'm too well-built for the costume. I guess Victorian maidens were slender and sexless.'

Lewis tried to sound interested in their day but all he wanted to do was take Harriet to bed and make love to her, just as he'd made love to Ella but this time with love and feeling. 'Did Oliver have a good time as well?' he asked.

'Sure, he wasn't that turned on by the historical part. He said all those costumes and the mud just made him grateful he was living in the twentieth century, but he sure enjoyed his trip into the copper mine.'

Harriet shivered. 'I didn't. It was freezing cold and I kept worrying about what would happen if the train broke down and we got stuck in the bowels of the earth.'

Edmund rested a hand on her shoulder for a moment. 'I'd have kept you warm,' he said softly, and Harriet turned her head to smile at him. Lewis's heart began to race and he quickly stood up.

'I'll ask Mrs Webster to make us some coffee,' he murmured.

'What did you do all day?' asked Harriet innocently when he came back.

'Spent a lot of time with Mark and then sat outside enjoying the good weather.'

'Where's Ella?' asked Noella sharply.

'She sat out for a bit but then said something about taking a bath and I haven't seen her since,' said Lewis smoothly.

'I must have a proper talk with her after dinner,' said Harriet. 'She hasn't mentioned breaking up with Simon yet, and I know she'll want to talk about it. At one time it looked as though they were going to get married.'

'I don't think her heart's really broken,' commented Lewis.

Harriet stared at him. 'How do you know? Has she discussed it with you?'

'No, but she seemed quite cheerful. It's a pity she can't swim,' he added.

'Why's that?' asked Harriet, who knew perfectly well that Ella could swim.

'A waste of the facility.'

Edmund nodded. 'I know what you mean. No strutting around in her bikini and no shared pleasures of the pool for our Ella.'

'Oh, she wore a bikini,' said Lewis with a grin. 'Quite a neat little number too.'

A warning bell sounded in Harriet's head. 'Has she talked to you about working in any of your films?' she asked.

'She's dropped a few hints, yes.'

'Just don't use the casting couch to try her out,' warned Harriet, smiling to hide her genuine fear.

'Why not?' asked Lewis softly. 'Does the thought of that disturb you?'

'It would sure as hell disturb me,' said Noella quickly. 'I'm popping over to Oliver's cottage,' she added. 'He seems to have walked off with my camera.'

'How convenient,' remarked Edmund. 'Come on, Harriet, show Lewis your picture.'

Harriet reached inside a carrier bag and drew out a framed sepia photo of herself dressed in Victorian costume. Lewis stared at it and felt his desire for his wife increase even more. She looked so innocent, so untouched, and yet her gaze was watchful as she stared out at him. With her long hair drawn back from her face she seemed both wary and trusting. Like a child, he thought, a child with a woman's body and mind.

'Good, don't you think?' said Edmund quietly. 'They put one up on display straight away, to trick other visitors into thinking they'd look as good. Noella's would have proved otherwise.'

'Noella looks fine,' said Harriet. 'I think you're being really unkind about her picture. No wonder she spent more time talking to Oliver than to you today.'

'He's more her type,' said Edmund in a matter-of-fact tone of voice. 'It's just a pity he isn't rich. If he were she'd run off and leave me and they'd live happily ever after.'

Lewis frowned. 'Where would that leave you?'

Edmund thought for a moment. 'Free,' he exclaimed with a laugh. 'Free to choose someone who'd suit me better as well.'

'That might not prove as easy as you think,' Lewis pointed out.

'It's easy enough,' retorted Edmund. 'I've already met someone. The trouble is, she's spoken for.'

Harriet looked from her husband to Edmund and knew that she had to get out of the room. She couldn't cope with the tensions and simmering anger that lay beneath the civilised façade they were both presenting. 'I'm going to find Ella,' she announced, and fled from the room.

'This woman,' said Lewis slowly. 'Do I know her?'

'Know her? That's a difficult question to answer. You're certainly acquainted with her.'

'Be careful, Edmund,' said Lewis quietly.

'I'll be as careful as you were this afternoon when you made love to Ella in full view of Mrs Webster. She was very shocked I'm afraid, and but for Noella's intervention just now would certainly have left.'

Lewis felt the blood drain from his face as Edmund turned and left him. Caught in the excitement of the moment, and needing to expunge the memory of the film of Harriet with Edmund and Oliver, he'd forgotten all about their housekeeper and her view from the kitchen window.

While the drama slowly unfolded inside Penruan House, Noella was enjoying a drama of her own. All day she'd longed to have Oliver make love to her once more, and at every possible moment the pair of them had touched or exchanged intimate glances as their mutual desire rose.

Now, in the safety of Oliver's cottage, they were both free to express their passion, and to Noella's delight she had no sooner set foot inside the hallway than Oliver had gripped her arm and hurried her through the main living area into the room that he used for working out.

They both tore off their clothes, silent but united in the excitement of the moment. Then, still without a word, Oliver lay on his back along his workout bench with his legs on each side, feet flat on the floor, and lifted his hands until they were gripping the end of the lateral bar.

His erection was vast, the veins standing out like blue ropes and the glans swollen and crimson. Noella didn't need any instructions; she knew exactly what she wanted to do and positioned herself above him, sitting astride his lower abdomen with her own feet also flat on the ground.

She sat with his erection trapped between her softly rounded belly and his own well-muscled abdomen and leant forward so that she too could grasp the lateral bar, her hands on Oliver's. This meant that her voluptuous breasts were dangling within reach of his mouth. Oliver's neck muscles strained as he drew her left nipple greedily into his mouth and began to suck hard on it.

'Graze me with your teeth,' Noella urged him. 'And suck harder – I like my men to be rough.'

Oliver needed no second urging. He nipped the edges of her sharply pointed nipples with his teeth and then opened his mouth wider so that he could suck in the surrounding areola as well.

Noella sighed with pleasure and rocked to and fro on him, stimulating herself between her thighs until she could feel the first tingles of arousal beginning deep within her.

Suddenly Oliver nipped a little harder at her breasts and as the searing heat-filled sensation darted through her she lifted her hips and very slowly eased his penis inside her. As soon as he was safely encased she squeezed her pelvic muscles and gripped him harder until he had to beg her to stop in case he came.

Reluctantly she released him a little and looked down at his sweat-covered face. 'I want this to be something we both remember,' she said in a low voice and Oliver pushed his hips up until she felt the end of his penis strike her cervix.

'So do I,' he assured her.

'Then keep still for a while, and leave it all to me,' she urged him.

Oliver shook his head. 'That's not my way.'

Secretly Noella was delighted. She liked a man to answer back, to take command even when she gave orders, but she also wanted sex with Oliver to be the kind she liked, and he saw the faint look of anxiety on her face.

'We're two of a kind, Noella,' he assured her. 'You're right, this is going to be great.'

Now Noella leant forward more and used the bar to pull herself up and down along his perfectly sculpted body. Oliver knew that she was managing to stimulate her entire pubic area with each pull. When she leant forward the penetration was deep and she would nuzzle his neck and nip the tender flesh beneath his ear before sliding back down him again.

Gradually the heaviness in his testicles turned into an ache and Oliver knew that he was very near. Before he could speak, Noella realised it too and she quickly changed her rhythm. Instead of moving up and down on him she began to rotate her hips from side to side which meant that the nerve endings inside her vagina were teased, sending delicious messages of arousal through her belly to her breasts, which were still being sucked hard by the diligent Oliver.

He'd never been so close to coming for so long and soon began to gasp with the effort of holding back as Noella continued her steady climb to orgasm. 'Soon,' she whispered, as her body started to tighten and he felt the involuntary tightening of her internal muscles as well.

Once this happened, Noella moved up and down even more slowly on him; he felt as though he were being tortured by an expert as his penis and testicles throbbed but he still wasn't given sufficient stimulation to climax.

Noella was breathing rapidly now and she drew back a little from her lover in order to see her nipples extended by his mouth. As her body rocked backwards onto the base of his belly and her breasts were fully displayed to him, Oliver knew that he could no longer keep control and he shouted a warning cry to Noella.

Swiftly she let go of the lateral bar with one hand, leaving her hand free to roam between her legs where it could massage her swollen and aching clitoris while at the same time she increased the tempo of her movements. In the end it was Noella who came first and she shouted, grinding herself hard against his hip bones and twisting her upper torso until he was forced to relinquish his hold on her glorious breasts.

Even as her last quaking movement began to die away, Oliver came too and his cry was even louder than Noella's as he finally released all the pent-up excitement and tension that had been kept at bay for what seemed an unbearable length of time. His hips jerked and his eyes closed as the spasms engulfed him, and looking down at him Noella knew with absolute certainty that this was a young man who would always be able to keep her happy.

When he was at last still, Oliver opened his eyes and smiled at her. 'Your turn to lie on the bench,' he said.

'What, now?' asked Noella incredulously.

'Yes, now, while you're still in the mood.

Quickly, lie like I was lying but with your feet right at the end of the bench.'

Her heart pounding with excitement at this unexpected turn of events, Noella changed places with him and to her delight he immediately crouched down on the floor at the foot of the bench and pulled her body towards him.

'First I think I need a drink,' he muttered, and Noella was about to protest when she realised that he was bringing a bottle of chilled champagne over to her. She heard it open with a loud popping sound and suddenly the ice-cold bubbles were flowing down across her exposed vulva, trickling into the crevices of her thighs and running down between her outer sex lips which were still open after the excitement of her previous orgasm.

Swiftly Oliver began to lap at the bubbles, opening her up with his hands and drinking from her in a way that even Edmund had never done before. 'You're beautiful here,' he said softly. 'I wish this could go on for ever.'

Noella wished that it could go on for ever as well. She felt him place a hand at the top of her pubic mound and then press down, pushing her clitoris closer to the opening of her vagina and at the same time increasing the feeling in her genitals. She shivered and as his tongue began to move gently over the clitoris she moaned, growing more and more excited as the sensations intensified.

After a time the regular rhythm became

unbearable as her needy body craved a change of stimulation in order to finally peak, and she thrust her hips up higher to increase the overall pressure.

'Faster!' she shouted, desperate for him to understand what she wanted. 'Please – move your tongue faster now.'

Oliver heard her, but instead of doing as she asked he slid a finger inside her and then pressed steadily against the upper part of the vagina, while at the same time drawing the throbbing clitoris between his lips and proceeding to suck steadily on it.

'Oh yes! Yes, stay right there!' shouted Noella, in a delirium of excitement, and this time Oliver obeyed her. His finger remained in place, pressing heavily against her internal passage, and his other hand bore down against her pubic area until she felt as though everything inside her was so tight that she'd burst if she didn't come, while all the time he continued to suck on the small sensitive nub trapped between his supple lips.

'I can't bear it!' screamed Noella as the melting heat continued to spread and jagged streaks of white-hot pleasure shot through her entire body. 'Hurry! Hurry!'

Oliver knew that he didn't need to hurry, that within seconds now she'd climax again, and he watched as her thighs shook and quivered and then suddenly she went rigid and silent and her eyes rolled back in her head as an almost unbearably intense climax gripped her body.

For a moment she held her breath, and then she released it in a long drawn-out exhalation of total satisfaction and Oliver lapped at the sweetness of her secretions escaping from the entrance to her vagina.

While he licked, Noella felt the pressure of his chin on her highly sensitive labia and to her astonishment this proved to be the trigger for yet another climax, less intense this time but bitter-sweet with a strange deep ache filling her vulva and belly as the muscular spasms shook her for the third time until she finally collapsed in a heap, gasping for breath.

Oliver ran a hand tenderly over her stomach and breasts as he stood up and then covered her with a light blanket. 'Rest for a moment,' he said quietly. 'You can't go back to your husband looking like that. What will he think?'

'He probably won't even notice,' said Noella. 'It's Harriet who occupies his thoughts these days.'

Oliver sat on the floor next to her and handed her a glass of champagne. 'Here, I saved some for you. Harriet? Isn't she Lewis's wife?'

'Yes, but Edmund wanted her, and what Edmund wants Edmund gets.'

'I don't think I'd risk trouble with Lewis James,' said Oliver. 'He looks as though he'd be a rather dangerous man to cross.'

'He is,' confirmed Noella. 'I think that's part of the attraction for Edmund, the danger of it all. There's so little that's forbidden these days that when he finally finds something that is, he has to go after it.'

'And Harriet?'

Noella frowned. 'I don't honestly understand why Harriet's become his lover. Personally I wouldn't risk losing Lewis if I were his wife, but I'm beginning to think that it isn't a risk as far as she's concerned.'

'Meaning what?' Oliver was puzzled.

'Meaning,' said Noella slowly, 'that both Lewis and Harriet may be playing with the rest of us for the sake of art.'

'Art?'

She sat up, glanced at her watch and climbed hastily off the bench. 'Is that the time? I must dash.'

'What do you mean, art?' persisted Oliver.

'Forget it, honey. I may be wrong, and even if I'm right there's nothing I can do about it now.'

'What about us?' asked Oliver. 'Are you only playing with me?'

Noella shook her head. 'No way, but right now I'm living in the present. We're on holiday and I'm having a great time. I'll think about it more deeply if and when the need arises, okay?'

'You're special to me,' said Oliver. 'I've never met a woman like you before.'

Noella smiled. 'Maybe not, but I'm a few years older than you are.'

'That doesn't matter,' protested Oliver. 'We're meant for each other, I know it.'

'Can you see me living in Cornwall in the

winter, sweetie?' asked Noella gently. 'I'm used to the sunshine and warmth of California, remember?'

'You'd adapt,' said Oliver firmly. 'I can tell you're adaptable, and if you were happy wouldn't it be worth having to turn the central heating up a little?'

Noella pulled on her clothes and shrugged. 'Let's just enjoy the moment, Oliver. You mean a lot to me too, but right now life's a little confusing.'

Oliver nodded. 'It's all right,' he said with a smile. 'I can wait. I'm good at waiting.'

His words were still going through Noella's head when she slipped into Penruan House and up the stairs to the bathroom she and Edmund used. No sooner was she in the bath than the door opened and her husband walked in. 'You look very flushed and relaxed,' he remarked, sitting on the bathroom stool.

'Must have been the sun at Morwellan Quay today,' she said, lifting a leg in the air and soaping it slowly and sensuously while he watched.

'Did you get your camera back?'

'Sure, it's on the bed.'

'Good, I'd hate to think of you having a wasted journey. What did you think of Lewis having his fun with Ella in full view of the good Mrs Webster?'

'I was surprised,' confessed Noella. 'Ella's nothing special, and it's clear that Lew still dotes on Harriet.'

'Still?'

'Despite her behaviour since we got here,' said Noella calmly.

'Your behaviour hasn't been exactly exemplary,' pointed out Edmund.

'You wanted me to sleep with Oliver.'

'Perhaps. He's certainly a well-built young man,' murmured her husband, idly trailing a hand in the bath water and splashing some suds over her breasts.

'How would you know?'

Edmund smiled, and it was one of the smiles that Noella hated. 'He helped me out the other night in a little exercise I'd planned. I was most impressed with him, too.'

'What did he do?' asked Noella.

'He helped me make love to Harriet,' said Edmund, and as Noella's eyes widened in shock he walked out of the room.

Later that evening, Lewis and Harriet were changing for dinner. Harriet was still chattering on about her day but Lewis was quiet, mainly because he didn't want to talk about what she'd done, he wanted to make love to her, but Harriet had made it clear that she wasn't in the mood.

'What do you think of this?' she asked, turning to face him as she fastened the buttons on a burgundy-coloured chiffon blouse that hung in handkerchief points tunic-style over matching pleated palazzo pants.

'You look very elegant,' he assured her. 'Personally, though, I prefer you unclothed.'

Harriet sighed. 'Lewis, please, I'm tired.'

'You didn't say that to Edmund.'

Her eyes flashed angrily but she kept her voice controlled as she clipped on long gold ear-rings and held a gold choker up against her neck. 'Why do you keep talking about Edmund? You wanted me to sleep with him, and you were the one who filmed it. Without that, you wouldn't have anything for Mark to write about, so why are you trying to make trouble?'

'I'm not making trouble,' said Lewis, knowing that he was. 'Surely it isn't unreasonable to want to make love to my own wife?'

'There, I'm ready,' announced Harriet, turning to face him again.

'You've put your hair up.'

'I thought it went with the outfit. Don't you like it?'

'It makes me want to take out the pins and watch it fall to your shoulders.'

Harriet felt a shiver of desire go through her. She wanted Lewis as much as he wanted her, but for some illogical reason she felt that it would be a betrayal of their love. While she was involved with Edmund, testing her sexuality with a man she didn't love, she felt she couldn't let Lewis make love to her as well. The two men were so different, the relationships so totally unalike, that combining them seemed impossible.

'It's Edmund, isn't it?' asked Lewis angrily.

Harriet nodded. 'Yes, it is, but not in the way you think. Lewis, this was all your idea, and now you've got to stand back and see the results of your plotting.'

'Are you in love with him?' asked Lewis, his voice anguished.

Harriet shook her head. 'No, I'm not.'

He stepped closer to her and drew a finger along the exposed bones of her neck. 'Do you still love me?' he whispered, his other hand cupping her buttocks and pulling her up against his body.

Without thinking Harriet responded. Her hips tilted towards him, and her head started to go back, but then just as he began to manoeuvre her towards the bed she twisted free of him. 'Yes, I do!' she shouted, almost in tears. 'But right now, I wish I didn't.'

'Then stop the game,' he said urgently. 'Tell me you want to stop and it will all be over. Damn Mark, and damn the script. I want you to do what you choose.'

She smiled sadly. 'I know. The trouble is I have to go on now.'

'Why?'

'To see how far he'll take me, how far it is I want to go.'

'It wasn't meant to be like this,' said Lewis, opening their bedroom door. 'It's far more complicated than I expected.'

Harriet lifted her chin and her eyes were cool. 'Yes, well, you didn't have to involve Ella did you?'

'Ella?'

'When I talked to her earlier I gained the

distinct impression that you and she had got on very well in my absence.'

'You're talking rubbish.'

'You mean you didn't have sex with her?'

Lewis didn't answer, but he didn't have to – his silence was enough to confirm Harriet's suspicions. 'Is this to pay me back for doing what you wanted in the first place?' she asked.

'No, it just happened.'

'I hope you both enjoyed it. Presumably this is the way you intend to audition all the girls for the role of Helena?'

'I don't do the auditions normally. Harriet, you invited Ella here.'

She laughed in disbelief. 'Yes, and you invited Noella but I don't imagine you've been sleeping with her as well. Don't blame me because you couldn't resist a beautiful actress. Did she remind you of Rowena?'

'No,' he shouted angrily. 'If you really want to know, she reminded me of you and when I was making love to her, when she cried out with pleasure, I was imagining that it was you.'

'How very insulting to both of us,' said Harriet as she walked out of the room.

The others were already in the dining room and as soon as Harriet and Lewis joined them they sat down and rang the bell for Mrs Webster. Noella, resplendent in a black and white striped trouser suit over a white camisole top, smiled at Harriet. 'Love the outfit, honey.'

'I wasn't sure it suited me,' confessed Harriet.

'I'm usually happier in dresses but palazzo pants are so comfortable.'

'And wonderfully easy to remove,' Noella pointed out just as Mrs Webster brought in the bowls of mushroom soup. Mrs Webster glanced quickly at Noella, averted her gaze from Lewis, and left as fast as possible.

'Oh dear, another goof,' laughed Noella.

Ella, who was looking very feminine in a simple A-line silk shift dress in a shade of blue that exactly matched her eyes and had a pattern of red and cream flowers on it, frowned. 'What do you mean, *another* goof?'

Noella gave her a tight smile. 'I mean that poor Mrs Webster's already had one shock today when she saw more than she wanted to out of the kitchen window after lunch. She was all for leaving until I produced a small financial inducement for her to remain.'

Ella's face didn't change and Lewis had to admire her acting skill as she looked straight back at Noella. 'What did she see exactly?' she enquired.

'I wasn't here, sweetie. I thought you might know.'

'Probably Lewis swimming nude in the pool. He's rather keen on that, isn't he, Harriet?' said Edmund smoothly.

She flushed, remembering the way Lewis had made love to her in the water early on in the holiday. 'If she's that easily shocked maybe we should have let her go,' she said with a smile.

'And what exactly is it that you do, Ella?' continued Edmund a little later when their soup bowls had been removed and they were eating one of Mrs Webster's casseroles.

'I'm an actress.'

'Yes, I know, but what kind of an actress. Classical? Modern? Television soaps or films?'

'In this country films are few and far between. I enjoy classical work but I earn most of my bread and butter money on television.'

He looked carefully at her and then across the table at Lewis. 'I should think the camera would love her, don't you agree, Lew?'

Lewis nodded. 'Certain to with those bones.'

Ella sat up straight in her chair. She pushed her hair back behind one ear in an unconsciously flirtatious manner and smiled her best smile at Edmund. 'I'm afraid it's only the camera that does at the moment.'

'Really?' asked Edmund. 'I find that difficult to believe.'

'I might be sick in a moment,' said Noella to Harriet in an undertone. 'What is your friend playing at?'

'She wants the film role,' said Harriet calmly.

'Helena you mean? Isn't that a little ambitious?'

'Ella's never lacked self-confidence,' murmured Harriet.

'Have you considered Ella auditioning for a part in *Forbidden Desires*?' continued Edmund, smiling back at Ella.

'I'm considering it at the moment,' said Lewis.

191

'However, since you're only one of the financial backers I don't really think your opinion is going to weigh very highly when I make my final judgement.'

'You back Lewis's films?' asked Ella.

Harriet turned to Noella. 'I hope she doesn't think she wasted herself this afternoon.' They both laughed and it was only when Edmund switched his cool gaze on to his wife that Noella managed to regain control of herself.

Edmund was intrigued by Ella. At first he'd dismissed her as simply another pretty face, but he was beginning to think there was more to her than that. She was clearly intelligent, and like Harriet she had an understated sexuality about her that intrigued him. However, unlike Harriet, he felt that she was a young woman who was more interested in her career and the world of acting than she was in meaningful relationships. She might not be as bold as Harriet, nor as willing to experiment, but she'd certainly fit into the kind of life he was envisaging for himself if he and Noella parted.

He still wanted Harriet, and would far rather have her at his side than Ella, but he was a realist. If Harriet was going to return to Lewis, if she found that emotionally Edmund held no attraction for her, then he would need someone else, someone so close to Harriet in looks and ways that she might even be able to play the character Lewis had based on her on film. It would be a compromise, but not a hard one to make, and he thought that it was worth his while developing their relationship a little.

After the meal, when they were sitting lazily in the drawing room drinking coffee and eating some of the delicious chocolate fudge from Polperro, he went and sat next to Ella. 'You made love to Lewis today, didn't you?' he said softly.

Ella glanced round the room but the others were all busy and no one was paying them any attention. 'Yes, how do you know?'

'Mrs Webster told my wife. Cornish house-keepers aren't used to that kind of thing you know.'

Ella smiled. 'She didn't have to watch.'

Edmund leant forward and rested a hand on her silk covered knee. 'I'd like to watch,' he confided. 'How would you feel about that?'

'Watch me with Lewis?' whispered Ella, stunned by his words.

'Yes.'

'But – I mean – he'd never agree. He probably won't ever make love to me again. I don't think he enjoyed it that much.'

'Suppose you're wrong and that I can persuade him, would you enjoy it?' persisted Edmund, his heart racing at the idea that was rapidly forming in his mind.

Ella hesitated. She wanted the role of Helena more than she wanted anything else, but the idea of having Lewis make love to her again and to do it in full view of this slim, attractive Englishman who had an undeniable magnetism of his own, was almost irresistible. 'Yes, I think I would,' she said at last.

Edmund nodded. 'That's exactly the answer I was hoping for.'

'I still don't understand how you'd manage it, or why you want to,' said Ella.

Edmund raised an eyebrow. 'Do you need to understand?'

'I suppose not.'

'Precisely. Now, if you'll excuse me, I must speak to Harriet.'

Ella watched him cross the room and perch on the arm of Harriet's chair. As they started to talk she saw the way Lewis studied them and recognised the hidden anger in the depths of his eyes. A shiver of fear ran through her and she threw a stole over her bare shoulders. She had the dreadful feeling that for the first time in her life she might be playing out of her league.

Chapter Nine

FOR THE NEXT week the unusually warm spell continued and the inhabitants of Penruan House swam, visited the tourist attractions and continued their slow erotic dance around each other. The tension in the air grew, particularly after Oliver started joining them in the evenings for a drink and the occasional game of pitch-and-putt.

Harriet found that her flesh was longing for Edmund's touch again. She and Lewis hadn't slept together since their argument and her natural sensuality, together with the remembrance of the way Edmund teased and tantalised her, meant that she was constantly aware of her need for sexual satisfaction.

Noella, who continued her visits to Oliver whenever possible, watched Harriet struggling to cope with her affair, and watched too the way Ella contrived to parade her undoubted charms in front of both men, flirting naturally and effectively as she strove to impress them.

Lewis observed everyone and passed his impressions on to Mark, but for the first time ever when making a film he wasn't happy. Certainly the situation was intriguing, and he could picture it very well on the screen, but from a personal point of view he was finding it very hard to cope and this unexpected weakness annoyed him. Unwilling to blame himself he turned his annoyance on Harriet, convincing himself that despite her denials she was slowly falling in love with Edmund.

As for Edmund, he out of all of them was gaining the most enjoyment from the situation, and the greater the sexual tensions within the group grew the more he schemed. By the end of their stay he was determined that either Harriet would leave Lewis for him or he would make Ella his. His wife, he knew, was lost to him, but even that was a source of relief. In fact, Edmund felt that he had nothing at all to lose if the present situation continued. However, Lewis could have told him that it never paid to be complacent.

On a hot Monday morning Noella and Harriet were lying by the pool drying off after a swim. They'd both been relatively silent since breakfast, each lost in their own thoughts, but suddenly Noella turned to the younger woman.

'You're having an affair with Edmund aren't you?' she said calmly.

Harriet reluctantly opened her eyes and turned towards Noella. 'Why do you say that?'

'Because I'm tired of pretending I don't know.'

'If you know, why ask?'

'Because I don't understand the reason behind it,' said Noella, spreading sunblock over her legs. 'Lewis is madly in love with you and far more attractive than Edmund anyway. Why risk your happiness for a casual fling?'

'You should ask Lewis that,' said Harriet bitterly.

Noella stretched out her limbs and gave a soft sigh of pleasure at the feel of the warm sun on her skin. 'I thought as much,' she said slowly.

'Meaning what?'

'It's all a game, isn't it? You and Lewis are using the rest of us as material for his next film. If I'd known I wouldn't have come away with you; it's rather like reading someone's private diary without permission, don't you think?'

Harriet sat up. 'Yes, it probably is, but he's using me just as much as he's using you. I'm beginning to think that I was wrong about Lewis. He doesn't really know what love is, or even life for that matter. All that concerns Lewis is his work.'

Noella shook her head. 'That's not true, honey. Lewis adores you, and he's suffering like hell over your affair.'

'But he instigated it,' cried Harriet. 'Don't you see? That's why he invited you both along. He knew that this would happen. He had a theory about people being unable to resist the forbidden and used us to prove it.'

'He couldn't force you into an affair,' said Noella mildly. 'Surely that was your choice?'

'But he knew I'd be unable to resist.'

'He couldn't have *known* – he suspected, sure – but he didn't know. Now you've proved him right and he doesn't like it one little bit. He probably feels you betrayed him.'

'But if I hadn't slept with Edmund, if I wasn't obsessed with him the way I am, then there wouldn't be a film would there?'

Noella laughed. 'Are you saying you did it just to give Lewis a script?'

Harriet fell silent. She suddenly realised that what Noella was saying was true. Of course she hadn't done it only for Lewis, she'd done it for herself, because Edmund had fascinated her and Lewis had given her the opportunity to follow up that fascination without feeling guilty. 'You mean, he never intended me to actually go ahead?' she asked.

'He probably thought you would, but deep down I bet you all the money I've got he hoped you wouldn't. Lewis isn't very secure in personal relationships, mainly because he's had so little practice. He and Rowena used each other, there was never any real affection there, only lust. You're different, and you've changed him. Perhaps that's not a good thing. Maybe as a director of *cinéma vérité* films he needs to be single-minded in his approach to life, but now that he's married to you he can't go back to being the person he was, so you could say he's caught between two stools.'

'I keep wondering how it's all going to end,' admitted Harriet uneasily.

'Lewis will either become a man obsessed with his art again or he'll stay human.'

'And what about me?'

'Either way you'll have learnt a valuable lesson, honey.'

'And what's that?'

'That most of us don't recognise a good thing until we lose it. My, look who's coming our way,' she added, and Harriet saw Ella walking towards them in a revealing swimming costume.

'Lewis still wants her,' said Harriet in a low voice.

'Most men would want her the way she looks and moves. Why did you ask her to join us?'

'We've been friends for years; I didn't realise what she was like when men were around.'

'She doesn't want Lewis,' said Noella keeping her voice low. 'She just wants the lead role in his film. Anything else is simply a bonus.'

'Noella,' said Harriet urgently. 'Are you in love with Oliver? Or is he just a bonus too?'

'He's neat.'

'That's no answer,' said Harriet crossly. 'I need to know. Do you love him, or are you still in love with Edmund?'

'I'm not in love with Edmund any longer,' Noella said quietly. 'I was at the beginning of the holiday, but I'm not now. I've grown tired of being what he wants. I think it's time I started being what I want instead.'

'And does that suit Oliver?'

'It seems to,' said Noella with a warm smile. 'It really does seem to.'

Harriet was pleased for the blonde woman, but before she could say any more Ella had sat down on the grass beside them. 'Have you swum already?' she asked brightly. 'I was hoping you'd race against me, Harriet. We used to have swimming races at our boarding school,' she explained to Noella. 'Harriet always won then, but I've been putting in a lot of practice over the years and I think I might be able to beat her now.'

'Does it really matter?' asked Harriet with a half-smile on her face as she remembered Lewis's comments about Ella's inability to swim. Clearly honesty was not her strong suit.

'If I beat you or not?' asked Ella meaningfully. Harriet nodded. 'Yes then, since you ask, I think it's probably very important.'

She didn't mean swimming and Harriet knew it. 'Ella, why are you doing this?' she asked in astonishment. 'We've been friends for so long, you could ruin it all.'

'I'm an actress and Helena is the role of the decade. As far as I'm concerned that comes before anything else,' said Ella. 'I'm sorry, Harriet, truly I am, but you know how much my work means to me, and it always has done.'

'You and Lewis should go very well together,' said Harriet bitterly and before Ella could reply she started running back to the house.

She collided with Lewis in the hallway and he

put his arms round her to steady her. 'Hey, what's the rush? Is someone after you?'

Harriet bit on her bottom lip to force back the tears that were unexpectedly filling her eyes. 'No, I'd had enough sun, that's all.'

'You feel hot,' he said softly, his cool hands roaming over her bare shoulders and upper arms.

'Lewis,' said Harriet, her legs almost collapsing with the strength of her desire. 'Let's go upstairs.'

'Are you sure?' asked Lewis, hardly daring to believe what he was hearing after the past week of abstinence.

'Yes.'

He needed no further encouragement, and a startled Edmund passed them on the stairs as they hurried up to their room, Lewis's arm round his wife's shoulder. Edmund continued on his way down and his mind raced. It was obvious that he must put his plan into action now, before Harriet was lost to him.

Lewis's hands stripped Harriet of her bikini in seconds and then he was fumbling with his jeans and short-sleeved cotton shirt, nearly tearing off one of the buttons in his haste. Harriet lay back on the large bed and watched him. The urgency with which he was tearing at his clothes and then the sight of his fully erect penis all increased Harriet's desire. Suddenly she couldn't understand why she'd been refusing him. It was clear now that sex with Edmund didn't mean giving up sex with Lewis. The two were compatible, and at this moment it was Lewis she wanted.

She lay on her back, her arms above her head and her legs parted as Lewis settled himself on her right, lying on his side. 'You're so lovely,' he murmured, stroking her just below her breasts and then round the tender underarm area. 'I've missed you these past few days.'

Harriet gave a half-smile. 'I've missed you too.'

She longed for him to start caressing her breasts, but Lewis was in no hurry. He continued to stroke the less obviously erotic areas of her body. Harriet was so eager for him that no matter where he touched her, her skin reacted with heightened pleasure and soon she was murmuring softly to herself.

Only when she was totally relaxed did Lewis bend his head and start to tongue softly at the rounded breasts, pushing them up towards his mouth with his hands and squeezing the undersides in slow, measured contractions.

Harriet moaned more loudly at the familiar pleasure. When he ran his unshaven chin across the tops of her breasts she almost cried out with happiness because it was one of her favourite actions and something that Edmund had never done.

As the voluptuous sensations increased, Harriet lifted her right leg so that Lewis could move his right leg under hers and over her left, his thigh crossing between her legs. She then reached down and took the soft vulnerable head of his erection in her hands, slipping it between her outer sex lips and moving it in small circles around her clitoris and the entrance to her vagina.

The result was incredible as a tight warm glow filled her entire pubic area, and she heard him give a low moan of desire as he strained to control himself long enough for Harriet to reach her first climax in this way.

She felt her clitoris start to swell and her lubrication increased as she continued to manipulate Lewis until finally the mass of nerve endings contained in that tiny nub retracted at the intensity of the feelings. Remembering Edmund's instructions, Harriet used her muscles to bear down hard and she felt the clitoris re-emerge so that she could now play the head of Lewis's penis up and down along the side of the clitoral shaft. This time the glow built higher and higher until she felt herself dissolving into spasms of ecstasy as her climax washed over her.

At the moment her contractions began, Lewis slipped the head of his penis into the entrance to her vagina and revelled in the feel of her body spasming around him, but still he managed to keep his own climax at bay, determined to save that for the next stage of their lovemaking.

Harriet looked at him and smiled. 'That was heavenly.'

'This will be even better,' he promised her, and then she felt him moving slowly inside her and as he moved so the pressure against her pubic area increased, caused by the weight of his thigh against her. She revelled in the sheer hedonism of the moment.

In this position it was almost impossible for Lewis to thrust too rapidly and easy for Harriet to dictate the pace, which she did by pressing with her legs to slow him every time he started to move faster than she wanted. It was frustrating for him, but in an exciting way, and the more his orgasm was delayed the more his desire for her increased.

It was the gentle movement of his upper thigh between her legs that really excited Harriet. She loved the feel of him inside her, but the added thrill of the weight against her increased the depth of the sensations that coursed through her, and as the pleasure mounted she became more and more abandoned, uttering cries of desire and urging him on.

Then, as always happened, her climb to orgasm abruptly took on a more rapid pace and she felt the pleasurable tingles start to tighten behind her clitoris and her breasts felt swollen and hard. She thrust them upwards, silently beseeching Lewis to pay them some attention and he reached for her nipples with his right hand, drawing the rigid little peaks away from the breasts and rolling them between two fingers before releasing them.

Now every part of her was alive and frantically surging to the point of no return. Harriet started to pant with excitement and at last she allowed Lewis to increase his pace and he thrust in and out of her more rapidly, and all the time he was pressing his thigh against her full and heavy pelvic area.

Harriet began to tremble as the first coiling sensations spiralled upwards through the centre of her body, and then Lewis's thigh pressed down more firmly still and sharp shards of almost painfully intense pleasure lanced through her belly and thighs while at the same time his long fingers squeezed her right breast tightly.

As he squeezed, Harriet's body finally reached its peak and she felt the fierce tightness explode into a shattering release, and once more her muscles spasmed helplessly in the blissful moment of satisfaction.

'Now it's my turn,' said Lewis thickly and she felt him moving deep inside her, until he too was shuddering and groaning as his body was finally allowed to climax and all the pent up tension and desire of the past week was released in the violent spasms of his orgasm.

Later, as they lay together, totally replete and happy, Harriet buried her head against his shoulder. 'I didn't want it to end,' she confessed.

'Perhaps it needn't,' suggested Lewis.

'What do you mean?'

'Why don't you let me put the vibrating loveballs inside you for the rest of the day,' he suggested. 'You know how easily you climax with those inside you. You could have orgasms all day in front of the others but only you and I would know.'

Harriet's pulse quickened. 'Yes, I'd like that,' she agreed, imagining how it would feel when the soft waves of pleasure washed over her in front of

Ella, Edmund and Noella.

'Edmund wants to talk to me later,' continued Lewis. 'I think he has an idea for some new night-time games. It seems that pitch-and-putt is losing its appeal!'

'What kind of games?' asked Harriet.

'Sophisticated ones I imagine.'

'Involving all of us?'

Lewis's arms tightened round her. 'Yes, involving all of us. I suppose I always knew what would happen in the end.'

'He hasn't said anything to me,' complained Harriet.

'He probably feels he needed to get my approval first. If I say yes, Harriet, will you want to go ahead as well?'

She felt a surge of excitement and despite what had just occurred between her and Lewis she felt desire rising again. 'Yes,' she said firmly. 'I need to go on with Edmund. I have to find my limit.'

'Even if the game involves us all?'

Harriet's grey eyes were thoughtful. 'What's the matter? Am I meant to say no? Do you want me to stop now?'

He shook his head. 'I want you to be true to yourself.'

'I don't want to lose you,' said Harriet fiercely. 'That won't happen, will it?'

'I seem to remember you telling me that if it did it would be my fault.'

'I know, but that isn't strictly true. You haven't forced me to do anything, and all that I have done

I've enjoyed. It's only that I don't want Edmund to become more important to me than he's meant to be.'

'We'll have to wait and see, won't we?' said Lewis, suddenly weary of it all. 'Don't let's talk about it any more. Shall I put the loveballs in now?'

Harriet murmured agreement and felt Lewis slip a pillow beneath her hips before crossing the room to fetch the balls. He covered them in lubricating gel and then gently opened Harriet up between her thighs, slipping the two balls, joined together by a piece of cord, inside her vagina. Then he closed her outer sex lips and carefully massaged the entire area of the vulva until she felt herself swelling beneath the forcibly closed flesh. As her muscles began to move with the delicious sensations so the balls started to vibrate within her in a tantalising rolling motion that swiftly brought about a sweet ache that made her long for another orgasm.

Lewis saw the expression in her eyes and laughed. 'No, Harriet! You'll have to let the balls do the work. Come on, let's get dressed and join the others. I'm sure a game of badminton on the lawn would help you enjoy yourself.'

By the time they'd persuaded Ella and Edmund to join them for a game, Harriet was almost frantic for some kind of more intense stimulation that would put a temporary end to the dull throbbing need she was experiencing as the loveballs brushed against her inner nerve endings and kept her constantly on the edge of an orgasm.

207

'Harriet and I will play you and Ella,' said Edmund, throwing the shuttlecock over the net to Lewis.

Lewis served first, dropping the shuttlecock short so that Harriet had to bend sharply to scoop it back up. At once the loveballs inside her rolled forward and the ache travelled up beneath her pubic bone, while transient tingles traversed her inner thighs. Flushed, she straightened up just in time to reach high for a lob thrown up by Ella. She jumped and the balls hit the top wall of her vagina, near her G-spot. Forgetting the shuttlecock, Harriet felt her muscles contract and suddenly a rippling climax went through her.

'You missed it!' said Edmund incredulously. 'Hole in your racquet?'

'Sorry,' said a flushed Harriet. 'I misjudged it.'

He saw the blush on her cheeks and the perspiration on her top lip and wondered what there could possibly be about a game of badminton that was sexually arousing.

As the game progressed, Harriet experienced more and more tiny orgasms, like the early warning tremors of an earthquake. She was grateful when it was over and she could leave the court.

'I've never seen you play so badly,' commented Edmund.

'I couldn't concentrate,' said Harriet truthfully.

'Perhaps you're missing me,' whispered Edmund.

Harriet nodded. She was, but the loveballs were proving a powerful distraction from even that.

All day Lewis went out of his way to choose activities that would keep Harriet aroused. They went on a pony ride, which meant she was constantly shuddering in bursts of sexual release, and they swam which mean that the water lapped against her vulva increasing the feelings within her.

By the end of the day she'd lost count of the number of times she'd climaxed, but she found that the more her body was aroused the more she desired stimulation. The gentle satisfaction and sense of being permanently on edge became an irritation as her desire grew for an explosive orgasm that would exhaust her craving body and put an end to its seemingly insatiable demands for more.

Lewis was constantly aroused too. He knew every time Harriet climaxed, and the knowledge meant that he was also on edge, his desire honed by her stimulation and gentle trembling moments of release.

When they finally sat down in the drawing room after dinner, Edmund had his suspicions about what was happening. He noticed that for the first time Harriet had chosen to sit on the floor to drink her coffee, and that she rocked absent-mindedly to and fro as she drank, her eyes shining and her skin glowing in a way that he knew was connected with sexual arousal.

Finally he sat on the floor opposite her and stretched out his legs so that the heel of one foot was resting between her upper thighs. Harriet looked quickly round the room and saw that everyone else was busy talking or reading. Without further hesitation she edged towards Edmund, ensuring that the heel of his foot, slid up her thighs beneath her skirt until it came to rest against the silk panties that covered her vulva.

Slowly Edmund increased the pressure of his heel and immediately he noticed Harriet's breathing becoming more rapid and to his surprise the pink flush of arousal appeared on her neck and upper chest, just above the scoop neckline of her dress.

'This is interesting,' he murmured, looking at his newspaper as he spoke in case anyone looked over to see what was happening.

Harriet tried to press herself against him more firmly but he withdrew his foot and only replaced it when she was still again. She couldn't remember when she'd last been so frantic for direct pressure against her vulva; the loveballs were moving insidiously inside her, tormenting her with their ceaseless stimulation. Her whole body was frantic for total satisfaction – satisfaction that only firm pressure around her clitoral area could provide.

Edmund flexed his big toe against the very spot that was driving Harriet mad and heard her draw in her breath sharply in response. As soon as he heard that, he teasingly removed his toe and a look of anguished need crossed her features. With a smile, Edmund allowed his foot to move once more and this time he used the ball of his foot to massage the area of silk that covered the entrance to Harriet's vagina while his big toe continued to rotate over the tissue surrounding the clitoris.

The sensations were exquisite for Harriet. At last the incessant clamouring of her flesh for greater pressure than the loveballs could provide was being satisfied and she felt her whole body tense and her legs began to quiver frantically beneath her skirt. Her mouth opened a little and she breathed slowly to try and control her vocal responses to the sheer bliss of the moment.

Edmund could see Harriet's nipples pressing against the fabric of her blouse and as her breasts swelled, the rounded tops rose above the confines of her bra and the creamy flesh was just visible to him as she bent forward a little in order to increase the sensations between her thighs.

After a whole day of tiny rhythmical contractions, of small but ultimately unsatisfying orgasms, the nearing climax felt to Harriet like an approaching earthquake whose early warnings had been ignored.

Her thighs and belly cramped painfully as her tight muscles drew in on themselves in preparation for the release Edmund's foot was promising and she heard a tiny whimper escape from her mouth. She looked about her but no one else seemed to have heard and she turned her attention straight back to what was happening to her increasingly wanton body.

Edmund had never seen her so flushed and her

211

eyes were wide with desire and fear that this moment of ecstasy might still elude her. Finally he judged that she simply couldn't wait any longer and he slid his toes up the outside of her silk panties, along the line of her sex lips, in order to press against the tissue around her throbbing nub of pleasure.

This was precisely what Harriet's aching flesh had yearned for and without any warning her entire body began to heave and shake as the long-awaited final orgasm crashed down on her. It was so intense, so utterly consuming with its shattering explosion of wild hedonistic pleasure, that she screamed with gratitude.

'Oh yes! Yes!' she sobbed. As the sensations became too great to bear, her muscles twisted her body forward in an uncontrollable contortion. 'That's bliss, such bliss!'

Edmund never took his eyes from her, and everyone else in the room turned to look as well, startled at the sudden outburst.

Neither of the other two women present knew how it had been brought about, but they were both very aware of what was happening and watched with fascination as Harriet continued to writhe and moan, her hair falling loose to her shoulders with a few strands clinging damply to her forehead and neck.

For Oliver, who'd been sitting playing cards with Noella, it was an unbelievable experience and he felt his mouth go dry and his penis stir at the sight of Harriet, gasping and ecstatic as she took her pleasure in full view of them all. If anything, it was even more arousing than when she'd been blindfolded and tied naked to his body, because then he hadn't been able to see her face or concentrate on anything apart from preventing his own climax.

Lewis, who understood very well what Harriet must have felt like by the end of the day, studied his wife in the throes of one of her most intimate moments of pleasure and realised to his surprise that this time he wasn't jealous.

She looked incredibly beautiful to him as her body finally stopped moving and she leant back against the chair, slowly regaining her composure. Not only beautiful to him, but also beautiful because of what the scene would look like played out on film. He could visualise it so clearly, the lingering shots of the foreplay that had led up to that moment of release, a moment that the cameraman would hold in tight close-up to capture every nuance of expression in her eyes. Only they wouldn't be her eyes, they'd be the eyes of the actress who played Helena, and at this thought he turned to look at Ella.

Ella was as turned on by it all as the men, and she parted her lips before moistening them with the tip of her small pink tongue. She too was physically aroused, and would very clearly be able to reproduce the scene she'd just witnessed. For the first time Lewis began to think that she might, after all, be given the role she craved so badly.

For Harriet, when the bliss of release had passed, it was the most awkward moment of her life. She kept her eyes on the ground for a long time before raising them to look at Edmund. He stared back at her, his mouth unsmiling but there was a light in his eyes that made his admiration and desire very plain. 'More coffee anyone?' he asked, getting to his feet in one swift easy movement.

'I could certainly do with some, honey,' exclaimed Noella, startled by Harriet's passionate outburst.

'Me too,' put in Oliver, who was now desperate to make love to Noella.

'I think I'll go off to bed,' said Ella, who was so stimulated by what she'd seen that she couldn't wait to get her hands on her vibrator and bring herself to orgasm. 'It's been a tiring day.'

'It certainly has,' said Lewis with a smile. 'What about you, Harriet? Are you thirsty?' She shook her head, unable to speak to any of them and wanting only the sanctuary of her room. 'Why don't you go up,' suggested Lewis, who guessed how she was feeling. 'I'll join you later. You can always watch a video or something.'

'I didn't know we'd got a video player,' said Noella.

Lewis nodded. 'I have, I always insist on having one installed in my bedroom wherever I'm staying. That way I can see clips or rushes as necessary.'

Edmund came back into the room with a pot of

coffee and some cups. 'Have you watched much since you got here?' he asked.

Lewis shook his head. 'Very little really, but what I have watched has been highly rewarding.'

'I'm sure it has. Actually, Lew, I wanted to have a private word with you if I could.'

'I think he wants us to go,' said Noella, downing her coffee in haste. 'How about a stroll along the lane, Oliver? It might help us sleep soundly!' Oliver didn't need asking twice and Ella left the room with them, leaving Edmund and Lewis finally alone.

'Something wrong?' asked Lewis slowly.

Edmund shook his head. 'On the contrary, everything's going very well. I can't remember when I last enjoyed a holiday so much.'

'That's nice to hear.'

'I really wanted to talk to you about *Forbidden Desires*.'

Lewis's eyes grew guarded. 'What about it?'

'Well, you've been spending a lot of time with Mark since we got here, I wondered how far on with it you were.'

'Pretty well on. If you're worried you can always drop out you know. I'm sure I won't have a problem finding backers.'

Edmund smiled. 'I'm sure you wouldn't, but I don't have any plans to back out. It's a simple enough question, isn't it?'

'Frankly I don't think it's any of your business,' said Lewis. 'You didn't ask any questions about *Dark Secret*.'

'Ah, well no,' said Edmund quietly. 'But that was different, wasn't it?'

'In what way, different?'

'I wasn't personally involved.'

The two men stared at each other in total silence, and it was a long time before Lewis spoke again. 'In what way, personally involved?'

'I have a suspicion,' said Edmund quietly, 'that I'm helping you write your script.'

'You can't seriously mean that,' retorted Lewis.

'I admit that it seems on the surface to be unlikely but yes, I mean it. Actually, it was Noella who first voiced the idea; it's only recently that I've decided she's right.'

'On what do you base that decision?' asked Lewis.

'On the fact that since you're neither blind nor stupid you must be aware of the fact that Harriet and I are having an affair. Now, I would have thought this would, at the very least, result in me being on the receiving end of a rather nasty blow to the nose. On the contrary, you're as amiable as ever and, rather tellingly, you seem to be continuing to make love to Harriet yourself. All of this would only make any kind of sense if the affair had been contrived by you. The mutual desire between Harriet and myself is, I rather think, forbidden. Your film title therefore fits the situation very neatly.'

'If you're right,' said Lewis carefully, 'what do you intend to do about it? Sue me when the film comes out? Quite difficult since you'd have to come clean about everything that's gone on at Penruan House since our arrival.'

'I wouldn't dream of suing you; I think it will make an excellent story. No, what I want to do is help you find an ending.'

'Suppose I already have an ending in mind?' asked Lewis.

'You don't,' said Edmund with total confidence. 'You can't have, since the film is *cinéma vérité* there is no ending until the situation here is resolved.'

Lewis leant back in his chair. His eyes were alert as his brain raced. 'Summarise the situation for me.'

'My wife no longer wishes to remain married to me and is having the time of her life with an athletic young Cornish bodybuilder. Your wife is broadening her sexual experiences with an enthusiasm which I find highly erotic and you yourself are having an affair with a young actress who wants the leading role in your film.'

'So what's your ending?'

Edmund shook his head. 'Not so fast, Lewis. Am I right in what I'm saying?'

'Possibly.'

'I'll take that as confirmation. Very well then, the truth is that I don't yet have an ending because I, like you, enjoy watching relationships run their course. It would spoil everything if I were to contrive an ending simply to suit me.'

'Then I fail to see how you can offer me an ending,' said Lewis shortly.

'It all comes down to the games I was telling you about,' said Edmund, leaning forward in his chair. 'I thought it would be fun if you and I, together with our respective holiday partners, had a small contest.'

Lewis frowned. 'What kind of contest?'

'On the first night we'd each see how many times we could bring our women to a climax before they asked us to stop. Or possible just how many times we could make them reach an orgasm, since one of them might try to put an end to it before the truth was known.'

'And then?'

Slowly Edmund smiled. 'Why then, on the second night, we'd change round. If, for example, I'd managed to bring Harriet to the pinnacle of ecstasy ten times on the first night, then it would be up to you to surpass that total within the same time span. The same rules would naturally apply to Ella.'

'And then what?' asked Lewis.

'Why then the man who does the best wins the prize.'

'There are two prizes.'

'No.' Edmund's eyes were cold. 'You and I know very well that there's only one prize at stake here and that's Harriet.'

'This presupposes that we both try equally hard on each night,' Lewis pointed out.

'I won't cheat,' said Edmund sharply. 'It hadn't crossed my mind that you might.'

'I wouldn't, it was merely a thought. And then

there's the question of the women. What if one of them fakes an orgasm?'

'Noella will watch it all very carefully. I think that women are more difficult to deceive than men where orgasms are concerned.'

Lewis thought that it would make an incredible ending, but didn't know if he was willing to risk losing Harriet in order to see the film resolve itself before his very eyes.

'Not afraid of losing, are you?' Edmund asked.

'Yes,' Lewis admitted. 'I am afraid, but it would make a fantastic ending.'

'And art comes before life?'

'Save the moralising,' said Lewis shortly. 'I've said the idea's sound. As long as all the women agree then the games can go ahead. When did you want to start?'

'Since Harriet is probably a little tired tonight and might need a day to recover, I think in two nights' time.'

'Do we warn the girls in advance?'

'Naturally, but I hardly think it's a warning,' said Edmund, smiling again now that he was certain he was going to get his own way. 'I'm sure they'll be positively eager to play.'

Lewis stood up and poured them both a drink. 'To the climax of the film,' he said with a short laugh as he raised his glass.

'To the prize,' said Edmund softly, and then he drained his glass in one go and walked swiftly from the room.

Lewis wondered uneasily what Harriet would

say if she knew that he had toasted his film while Edmund had toasted her.

Chapter Ten

'*ARE YOU NERVOUS?*' Noella asked Harriet as they took an evening stroll round the grounds of Penruan House half an hour before the first game was to begin.

'Not really,' confessed Harriet. 'I thought I would be, but now that the moment's here I'm excited. I kept looking at Edmund today and imagining what it was going to be like to have him making love to me while Lewis watched.'

'You'll have to watch Lewis make love to Ella as well,' Noella pointed out.

'I don't think I'll have a problem with that, not if I'm caught up in the sensations Edmund's causing, but then again, who knows? Maybe I'll hate seeing Lewis with her.'

'It's strange,' said Noella thoughtfully. 'When we were driving down here at the start of the holiday, I had this terrible fear that I was going to lose Edmund to you and I was determined to fight for him. Once we were here, and I met Oliver, I realised that he wasn't worth fighting for any more. Whatever we once had must have gone some time ago, only I never realised. Do you think that you might come to the same conclusion about Lewis?'

'No,' said Harriet firmly. 'Lewis is worth fighting for, but I don't have to fight for him. I know he still loves me.'

'And do you still love him?'

'I think I do. I just hope that the next two nights don't change my mind.'

'May I give you a word of advice, honey?' asked Noella.

Harriet smiled. 'Of course.'

'Don't make the mistake of falling in love with Edmund. You may get annoyed by Lewis's passion for his work, but at least he's got passion. Edmund has desire and incredible technique but no passion. Even if you did love him he'd never love you back, not in the way you deserve. He simply isn't capable of it.'

'And Oliver's different?'

'Completely different in every respect. I just wish he'd agree to come and live in the States, but he won't. Oh well, we'd better go back. It's time you were getting yourself ready.'

Once in her own bedroom Harriet hesitated, unsure what to wear for the night's entertainment. She rejected obviously sexy outfits as being too blatant, sensing that Edmund's taste would run to more sophisticated clothing. Finally she settled on a navy blue silk negligee set with white hold-up stockings and a tiny navy G-string beneath. After bathing and putting on her make-up, she sprayed herself with perfume and then checked her hair.

As she piled it high on the top of her head and then pulled down a few strands at the front to form a long fringe that emphasised her eyes, Lewis came into the bedroom. He gave a sigh of pleasure. 'You look wonderful, Harriet. Utterly intoxicating. I wish it was my turn tonight.'

'I'm sure Ella will look just as desirable,' Harriet said calmly, but her heart was starting to race wildly now that the moment was actually so close.

'No doubt,' agreed Lewis, trying to still his own fears about what the night might demonstrate. 'You really want to do this, don't you?' he added.

Harriet nodded. 'Oh yes. This way I'll find out all that I need to know about myself.'

'We'd better go up then,' said Lewis slowly. 'Kiss me first, Harriet.'

They moved into each other's arms and their mouths met in a slow lingering kiss that threatened to turn into something more until Harriet forced herself to pull away. 'A kiss for remembrance?' She laughed unsteadily.

'A kiss for luck,' he said huskily. 'I have a feeling I'm going to need it before the next two nights are over.'

'Go and fetch Ella,' said Harriet. 'I'll join Edmund. He should have everything ready by now.'

She was right. The light bulbs in Edmund's bedroom had been changed and were now coloured, their glow soft and flattering. Scented candles burned in holders around the room and through the open bathroom door Harriet could see that he'd done the same in there.

The room was very warm but he'd left the top window open so that any breeze would refresh them should it become too hot.

'Very nice,' said Harriet approvingly.

He handed her a glass of champagne and then dipped a baby sweetcorn in a yoghurt dressing before holding it up to her lips. Harriet nibbled delicately at it until her mouth felt the touch of his fingers as she took the final piece from between them. Gently Edmund ran his finger beneath her bottom lip to remove a tiny speck of dressing and then he raised his own glass to her.

'Here's to an exciting evening, Harriet.'

Her eyes danced over the rim of the crystal goblet. 'To an exciting evening,' she echoed just as the other two joined them.

Ella's choice of clothing had been less subtle than Harriet's, but Harriet had to admit the effect was very sexy. She was wearing a black and white striped basque that pushed her breasts invitingly upwards, black silk french knickers, a pearl choker and matching pearl ear-rings, while her tanned legs were smooth and bare, their shapely calves accentuated by the black stilettos she was wearing on her feet.

Lewis looked from his wife to Ella and realised

that they both excited him in their different ways, and he could tell from Edmund's expression that he felt the same. Ella's hair had been left loose and as a result she looked younger than Harriet, less sophisticated and more vulnerable, whereas the truth – and both men knew it – was quite the opposite.

Ella and Lewis were handed their goblets of champagne and then Lewis fed tiny carrot sticks covered in the dip to Ella while Harriet watched. However, Lewis didn't caress Ella's mouth and although the actress managed to lick quickly at the tip of his finger, it was clear that as yet the sexuality between the two of them didn't equal that between Edmund and Harriet.

'Shall we start in the bathroom?' suggested Edmund. 'I have one particular device that I'm sure Harriet will enjoy which needs the bathroom, and besides, it's always nice to freshen up together before we begin in earnest.'

Lewis nodded, and moved towards the open door. To his surprise Edmund paused to take Harriet in his arms and then he began kissing her gently round her neck and ears while his hands unfastened the navy peignoir, so that he was able to remove it from her unresisting body and lower his head to where her breasts peeped above the lace covering of the slim strapped nightdress beneath.

Watching him tongue at the smooth uppersides of his wife's breasts, Lewis was seared by desire and quickly turned to Ella, his hands grasping her round her tiny waist as he urged her compliant body closer to his before allowing his mouth to roam in a similar fashion around the already exposed tops of her breasts and the highly sensitive skin beneath her arms.

By the time they were released, both women were flushed and breathing rapidly, and when Harriet felt Edmund's arms slip beneath her so that he could pick her up and carry her through to the bathroom she relaxed against him, her whole body open and throbbing with excitement.

She was vaguely aware of the fact that Lewis had gone into the shower cabinet with Ella and guessed that he was washing and arousing her there, but her attention was focused on Edmund and what he intended to do.

Very softly, Edmund eased the straps of her nightdress down over her arms, kissing every inch of the exposed skin as he went, and then at last her breasts were free and she shivered as he tongued at the rigid nipples. Then he picked up two transparent cones from the bathroom stool and eased them over her burgeoning flesh, before taking hold of the extending tube and fastening it to the cold tap over the basin.

As he worked he was murmuring to her, gentling her with the tone of his voice and the occasional touch of his hands, and so when he turned on the tap and her breasts were suddenly bombarded with jets of ice-cold water, she gasped with surprise. Before she could move, Edmund had pressed her down onto the stool and held her there so that she had to sit and let the spray continue to massage her aching tissue as the breasts swelled and hardened with the stimulation.

Finally, when she felt that she couldn't stand any more, he turned off the tap and carefully peeled off the cones to reveal two firm swollen globes with their nipples standing out proudly red and hard. Quickly he picked up a beaker, rinsed his mouth in hot water and then lowered it to the cold tingling breasts.

At the touch of his warm tongue and the pressure of his warm mouth against the freezing flesh Harriet gave another gasp, but this time of delight rather than shock; the contrast in temperature was so exciting that to her astonishment she felt herself quivering and shaking as a tiny climax swept through her.

Edmund nodded in satisfaction, pulled her to her feet and eased the nightdress off over her head until she was totally naked in front of him. 'Undress me,' he said in a low voice, and as she started to obey she realised that Noella was standing in the doorway.

'Did you see her come then?' Edmund asked his wife.

'Yes,' murmured Noella, fascinated by the sight of the slim, aroused body in front of her. 'She seems very sensitive.'

'Deliciously sensitive,' agreed Edmund as Harriet removed all his clothes. 'Now lie down in the bath,' he murmured. 'I want to do the same between your thighs using the shower head that's fixed to the taps.'

'Not the cold water first!' protested Harriet.

'But of course; otherwise the whole experience is changed. Lie back now, and open your legs for me.'

He'd placed a pile of towels in the bottom of the bath and Harriet lay back against them, her body shaking in anticipation of what was to come as he detached the shower fitment from its wall hanging. He was about to start the spray when Lewis and Ella emerged from the shower cubicle.

'Any success?' asked Noella.

'Not yet,' said Lewis. 'It was very agreeable foreplay though.'

'Harriet's already had one orgasm,' said Noella, and saw the brief flash of anger in Lewis's eyes. 'Watch carefully,' she continued. 'I think she's about to have another.'

Harriet was trembling violently as she waited, every muscle tense, for the onslaught of the ice-cold spray on her tender vulva, but at the same time she found that the flesh there was tingling with desire and her outer sex lips had parted in anticipation of the pleasure that was to come.

'Close your eyes,' said Edmund. 'That way it will be more of a surprise.' Harriet closed them and waited. Nothing happened. She could hear Lewis's breathing, Ella's muffled sounds of excitement at whatever he was doing to her and Noella's whispers but Edmund made no sound at all. She wanted to open her eyes, to see for herself what was happening, but her body told her to stay as she was. With every passing second her desire was heightened until she was in a fervour of suspense and, without realising it, she parted her thighs still more.

Edmund smiled and aimed the shower head carefully so that the cold water sprayed directly on the centre of her vulva, covering her most sensitive nerve endings and causing her to utter a cry of surprise before she adjusted to the sensation.

Once more Edmund judged his moment well and only when Harriet started to feel that the cold was too intense did he change the temperature of the water, and then she felt tepid water soothe and caress her straining tissue. Gradually, though, the tepid water changed as well until it became warm, and the heat turned her lower body into a fevered boiling mass of desire that had her thrusting her hips upwards as she cried out for the release of another orgasm.

Lewis, who was carefully stimulating Ella between her buttocks with soapy fingers, could hardly concentrate because of the gasped entreaties of his wife as she abandoned herself totally to the moment. At last the water did its task and once more her body shook beneath the onslaught of another climax so that she slumped back in relief against the towels.

'Two,' said Noella levelly, and as she spoke Ella whimpered with pleasure as Lewis's soaped fingers brought her to her first climax of the night.

After both young women had had a few minutes to recover they returned to the bedroom. Lewis chose to sit Ella down in the armchair by the window and Harriet saw him crouch down on the floor between her legs, and imagined only too well how his tongue would feel on the other girl's excited flesh.

Then Edmund drew Harriet gently over to the bed and placed a bolster down the middle of it.

'Lie face down on that,' he whispered. 'I want you to stimulate your own clitoris by wrapping your legs around the sides and pressing down with your hips. While you're doing that I'm going to penetrate you between your buttocks, you should find the combination intriguing to say the least.'

Now that he was beginning to move into darker areas, Harriet felt her body glow even more and she hurried to press her hungry flesh against the white bolster, grateful for the touch of the starched linen cover against her breasts and belly.

Edmund watched her bend her legs at the knees and grip the sides of the bolster as he'd instructed, and then his own excitement mounted as she began to move her body up and down and her hips round in circles as the demands of her clamouring body drove her on.

For Harriet the soft tickling feelings that at first resulted from her movements quickly changed into tingles that crept over her entire body, prickling and teasing her aroused flesh until she was hot with need. She felt her clitoris swell and

230

ground down more fiercely against the bolster, trying to reach the elusive climax, but she needed more and when she felt Edmund's hands on her hips slowing her down she gave a cry of gratitude.

Edmund covered her buttocks with a special gel that heated as well as lubricated the flesh and soon the warm glow was spreading over the perfect mounds and seemed to Harriet to be spreading through the skin to her internal organs as flames of hot desire smouldered within her.

Edmund watched her spasmodic movements with the eyes of a connoisseur and when he judged the moment right he covered the head of a small anal plug in the same gel, parted the glowing cheeks of her bottom and slipped the head into the tiny puckered opening.

For a moment Harriet was still, feeling the object sliding into the tight opening and allowing her muscles to relax in order to accommodate it. But then, without any warning, the hot glow that had heated her externally was filling her rectum, igniting the incredibly sensitive nerve endings there with an unquenchable fire that rushed through her belly and on upwards towards her breasts, until she started crying out and writhing harder against the bolster in her desperate search for release.

Satisfied that the plug had eased the way for him, Edmund slipped a protective sheath over his swollen penis and then withdrew the plug. For a moment Harriet felt bereft, empty in the place that most needed to be filled, but then he was easing himself into her and she gave a muffled sound of protest because he felt too large, too thick for the confined space.

Edmund slowed, reaching beneath her and allowed the middle finger of his right hand to flick at her damp protruding clitoris. He flicked several times and each time she shuddered convulsively as the scorching pleasure seared through her.

Confident that she could now accommodate him, Edmund continued to ease his way into her most secret opening until he was finally fully inside her and felt the tightness of the heated walls of her rectum close about him. Very gently he began to move and Harriet's arms reached out above her head as she strained towards the peak that was now incredibly near.

Her body had never felt so alive and when Edmund suddenly changed the rhythm of his movements and allowed himself two swift thrusts that were almost brutal it proved the trigger for Harriet's climax and she felt as though a fireball had exploded deep within her belly and the resulting flames scorched through every particle of her body.

'I can't bear it!' she screamed. 'It's so good, so good!' Edmund continued to move, to keep the fevered flesh at the point of ecstasy for as long as possible and Harriet continued to shout and shudder for several seconds until finally she was still.

'Definitely an orgasm,' said Noella, her voice uneven at the sight of Harriet's absolute abandonment to her body's satisfaction. 'That's three already.'

'The night's still young,' laughed Edmund, stroking Harriet's sweat-streaked back. 'I'm sure Harriet has plenty more where that came from.' Harriet, exhausted and shaking, wasn't so sure.

It was taking Lewis much longer than he'd anticipated to bring Ella to a second orgasm. He knew that he wasn't doing as well as he should, that his concentration wasn't focused on her but on the sounds emanating from Harriet, sounds of such intense delight that he could hardly bear to be in the same room as her.

Ella was doing her best to help, straining for a second climax that she wanted as much as Harriet had wanted hers, but for some reason she too was finding it difficult to concentrate. She realised that it was because she could hear Edmund's cool commands and urgent movements and wanted to be the recipient of his attentions herself, despite the fact that Lewis was the man she'd wanted when she arrived.

After a time, Edmund turned Harriet over and looked down at her flushed face. 'Incredible, just as I'd pictured it! Wait there, I think you need something to refresh you next.'

While he was out of the room Harriet watched the back of her husband's head and saw Ella's face contort into a spasm of pleasure as she at last shuddered in the throes of a second orgasm.

'How many is that for her?' Harriet asked Noella.

'It isn't a competition, at least not between you two,' responded Noella. 'You concentrate on what Edmund's doing.'

Harriet ran her hands down the sides of her belly and shivered. She felt totally free, her body tight and anxious for further stimulation from Edmund and yet she knew that no matter how intense the last orgasm had been, something was still missing.

Returning with a bowl of kitchen salt and a bottle of perfumed oil, Edmund removed the bolster from the bed and put down a sheet instead. Then he lay Harriet face down and mixed the salt and oil in the palm of his hand. 'I'm going to give you a massage,' he said quietly and gently glided his hands up and down her body on each side of her spine. The salt was coarse and her skin quickly began to glow again. She started to twist against the sheet but he stopped her with a swift stinging flick of his fingers on her bottom. 'This time you keep still,' he said shortly.

At first that wasn't too hard, but when he began to work on the insides of her thighs and up over the buttocks she could hardly contain herself, then when he slipped a finger between the cheeks of her bottom she bore down anyway, to ease the ache in her pelvis.

'I told you not to move,' said Edmund in a detached voice, and all at once she felt a sharper stinging sensation across her upper thighs as he used the damp end of a towel to chastise her. The slight pain startled her and to her shame she felt the tightness behind her pubic bone dissolve into an unexpected bitter-sweet orgasm that was impossible to disguise. 'Four,' called out Noella, and Lewis felt his blood run cold.

Harriet heard Edmund give a low laugh and then he was turning her over. His fingertips, covered in the mixture of salt and oil, were circling each of her breasts in turn, pressing the crystals of salt firmly into the skin and then finally brushing the textured mixture across her nipples themselves which tightened and seemed to shrink as the surrounding areolae swelled.

Edmund made his way down Harriet's body, lying next to her on the bed as he kneaded the muscles of her stomach and the sides of her body before covering her legs, finishing with her feet, rotating his fingers round on the pads beneath each toe until her pelvis and groin muscles began to spasm in a reflex action which Noella recognised only too well.

'Shall I rinse you off now?' he asked quietly.

Harriet's restless body lurched at the prospect. 'No, I want to come first,' she pleaded, and heard his sigh of pleasure at her response.

'Where do you want me to touch you next, then?' he asked, still massaging her left foot.

'Between my thighs,' she moaned, wondering how much longer she could stand the unendurable heaviness that was filling the whole of her pelvic region and making her vulva swell and ache.

'I will, but first I want to blindfold you,' he

whispered, and before she could protest the black silk band was over her eyes and she was being helped from the bed until she was standing sightless on the floor, her naked back pressed against his front with his erection nudging against her buttocks.

He let her relax against him for a moment and then suddenly pulled her arms around behind her back, gripped them in his right wrist and pushed her forward from the waist by pressing his left hand against the nape of her neck. She felt utterly in his power, vulnerable and excited at the same time, and her body shook slightly. 'You've no idea how much this turns me on,' Edmund whispered against her ear and then he planted a kiss on her spine just below where he was gripping her neck and her trembling increased.

Then, as suddenly as he'd pinioned her, he released her and now she found herself forced to the ground, kneeling with her thighs spread and the lower half of her legs outside his. 'Cup yourself between your thighs,' he insisted. 'Use your own hands to press against yourself.'

'I want you,' whimpered Harriet.

'Do as I say,' repeated Edmund, and slowly the sightless Harriet's hands strayed between her thighs until her palms could cup the tender ache and press against the needy flesh. Edmund kissed the side of her neck, and Harriet's head moved back to allow his mouth to travel more freely around her ears and jawline. As he kissed her she felt his hands insinuate themselves under hers and then he was moving her hands, pressing upwards so that her clitoris began to throb and then easing the pressure until the flames of desire started to abate a little.

He maintained this tormenting rhythm until Harriet grew frantic as her overheated body screamed for its climax. She felt as though all her insides were cramping as they were constantly drawn tight and then relaxed again due to the stimulation but at last he circled his hands against hers. This meant that the whole of the area beneath her outer sex lips was stimulated in the way she liked best and the throbbing of her clitoris increased in tempo until a searing flash shot through her, lancing up the middle of her body between her breasts and across her neck and shoulders as she erupted once more into a shuddering orgasm.

'There,' said Edmund calmly. 'Wasn't that worth waiting for?'

The blindfold was removed and he took her into the bathroom and led her into the shower cubicle before letting the warm spray cover them both. As the water cascaded down, he sponged every trace of salt and oil from her skin and then dried her briskly with a warm fluffy towel from the heated rail.

'I don't think I can come again yet,' murmured Harriet, walking ahead of him back into the bedroom.

'Of course you can,' retorted Edmund. 'This will help. Look, I had Oliver set up his exercise bike in the corner before we began. You'll find it a very stimulating piece of equipment used my way!'

Suddenly the room was filled with the sound of Ella's cries. Harriet turned and saw the young actress sitting on Lewis's lap, her legs wrapped round his waist and her head thrown back in orgy of excitement as he brought her to orgasm on his massive erection.

'Was she faking that?' Edmund asked Noella with interest.

Noella smiled. 'Certainly not!'

'Then it sounded very good, don't you agree, Harriet?'

Harriet did agree, and she found that simply watching and listening had brought her senses alive again, although she still felt too weary to contemplate another climax. Edmund, it seemed, did not intend to be guided by her judgement.

'Sit on the side of the bed and part your thighs, Harriet,' he said briskly.

'Why?'

'Just to allow me to put this inside you. It's an ivory phallus that I bought when I was out East once. Noella says it feels very agreeable. I'll be interested to hear if you agree with her.'

Harriet looked down and watched as he covered the phallus in jelly and then slowly eased the full length of it inside her vagina. It was very long and wide and at first slightly uncomfortable but once she was used to it she agreed with Noella, and its coolness was welcome after all that had gone before.

At the bottom of the phallus was a T-bar that kept it in place when Edmund removed his hands. He then pulled her to her feet and across to the exercise bike. 'Now, sit on the saddle, which is tilted slightly forward as you can see, and start to pedal. Try and keep your speed up, it will increase the sensations. The faster you move the greater the sensations.'

As soon as she was seated, Harriet realised what he meant about it being stimulating. The ivory phallus within her pressed against her vaginal walls, and the movements of her legs combined with the friction of her vulva against the saddle meant that every part of her vagina was titillated, and the nerve endings around the clitoris were also indirectly stimulated so that soon her belly began to swell and she felt her own lubrication seeping out onto the T-bar.

She was aroused and orgasmic, but sheer exhaustion seemed to prevent her from reaching the desired pinnacle and after a few minutes her legs moved more slowly on the pedals. 'That's not fast enough,' said Edmund.

'I'm tired,' retorted Harriet.

'You won't climax if you don't keep going.'

'Perhaps I've had all the orgasms I can,' she cried.

'Nonsense,' said Edmund, and behind her back he picked up a latex pleasure whip.

Harriet crouched low over the handlebars, trying to bring satisfaction to her screaming flesh and all at once she felt Edmund bring down the whip with searing force against her curved back. She shouted out in shock.

'Every time you slow the pace I shall strike you again,' said Edmund.

Harriet knew that she could stop the game, get off the bike and say it was over for the night, but a darker part of her didn't want that to happen. She wanted to be driven on, beyond the boundaries she would have selected for herself and so she kept going, and every time she slowed, every time her aching calf muscles tried to rest, the latex whip would strike her in what she now thought of as a special kind of caress.

The burning sensations from the latex whip joined up with the red-hot flickers from all the nerve endings stimulated by the ivory phallus until at last, just when she was despairing of relief, the whip fell one last time and she doubled forward and then jerked upright throwing herself back, forcing Edmund to catch hold of her to prevent her from falling off the bike as she was shaken by a cataclysmic explosion.

'There,' said Edmund softly as he removed the phallus, 'I knew you could do it.'

On shaking legs, Harriet went and sat on the bed and it was only then that she realised that Lewis and Ella had finished and were both watching her. Ella looked envious and astonished, but Lewis's expression was unfathomable.

'One more,' said Edmund to them all. 'She'll have one more and that I think will be the finish for tonight.'

'I can't!' said Harriet, but deep down she knew she was prepared to try.

'Yes you can, my love,' he assured her and she was so startled by the endearment that she lay back on the bed without further protest while Lewis, who had also heard it, had to restrain himself from physically attacking his one-time friend and financial backer.

Very carefully and deliberately, Edmund spread-eagled Harriet's legs, opening her up fully until everyone in the room could see the area between her thighs. Lewis saw that she was fully aroused, the outer sex lips flattened outwards, the clitoris enlarged and protruding proudly, and on her pubic hair the tell-tale signs of moisture from her vagina. Her breasts were full, the veins showing clearly beneath the skin and her nipples hard in the dark and swollen areolae.

Lewis, who had just climaxed deep within Ella, felt his scrotum tighten and his testicles lift towards his body, but Edmund, who had not yet allowed himself the luxury of an orgasm, had a full erection and his nipples were almost as erect as Harriet's.

Noella, the only one of them who had not been physically touched during the evening, began to stroke her breasts through the material of her figure-hugging dress. She wished that it was all over so that she could run to Oliver and let him assuage her starved senses.

'Hold her ankles,' Edmund told Noella. 'She

241

may move involuntarily otherwise and I don't want to lose her at the vital moment.'

The sight of the other woman, lying sprawled on the bed totally open to her gaze, aroused incredible feelings in Ella. She longed to be allowed to go forward and touch the clearly excited flesh herself, to swirl her finger against the button standing so proudly in the midst of the damp tissue but she knew that she had to stand and watch, allowing Edmund to draw forth what would have been for Ella an impossible final orgasm.

When Edmund's finger slid up her inner channel Harriet jumped. Her flesh was ultra-sensitive now and every movement threatened to be too intense unless carefully judged, but she trusted his skill as a consummate lover.

Very carefully he eased the finger inside her and massaged the area around her G-spot until he felt the tiny gland start to swell beneath his manipulations. Harriet felt it too and suddenly she was even more damp between her thighs as her body seemed to melt into a pool of liquid. It was an amazing sensation, far more intense than at any other time, and it made her wanton body crave the ultimate pleasure yet again, despite the fact that she was almost utterly exhausted.

Edmund massaged the G-spot for several seconds and then allowed his thumb to move up towards the clitoral area at the same time as he continued the internal caress. Now all the lubricated tissue was swollen, and as the glorious moment of climax approached, the previously proud clitoris retracted beneath its hood and some of the wonderful feelings died.

'No!' cried Harriet despairingly.

'Don't worry, relax and trust me,' Edmund soothed her as he pushed the hood up with his free hand, but the clitoris was too sensitive to be touched and when he tried to massage the shaft Harriet shifted uncomfortably.

She was almost out of her mind with longing now. Despite everything her nerve endings clamoured for this final orgasm. Already teased towards fulfilment she felt that she'd go mad if she wasn't allowed what she sensed would be the most intense experience of her life and yet her body was betraying her.

'I can't!' wailed Harriet.

'Of course you can,' Edmund assured her, allowing the clitoris to retreat once more. Then, still massaging her G-spot, he pushed the surrounding flesh upwards until he'd exposed the opening to her urethra, an almost invisible opening that he knew contained more nerve endings than any other part of the vulva. 'In a few more seconds, you'll come,' he whispered as he lowered his head.

Every part of her was as swollen and aroused as it could possibly be and the ache of unsatisfied desire was so intense that it was all she could feel as it throbbed deep within her belly and behind her pubic bone. 'My breasts!' she complained, feeling the heavy ache behind her nipples as well.

'Squeeze them yourself,' said Edmund, unable to help her himself. 'Start now, and squeeze harder than you'd normally squeeze.'

Gasping and moaning, Harriet encircled her breasts and squeezed. Immediately the ache changed into a thrill of wonderfully searing pleasure and, as she arched her hips slightly, with satisfaction Edmund finally allowed the very tip of his tongue to skim across her urethral opening and then flicked the point hard against the entrance itself.

Harriet's scream as her body jackknifed on the bed would have been heard by anyone in the house, and it even carried through the open window to Oliver's cottage where he sat reading in the tiny front room.

Noella kept hold of Harriet's legs so that Edmund could continue to play his tongue over this exquisite area of tender flesh and Harriet screamed again as the sensations continued to flood over her, finally quenching the previously insatiable hunger that Edmund had aroused in her.

'Stop!' she shouted at last. 'Let me go! That's enough, it's enough!' Lewis saw her roll around the bed in a final delirium of ecstasy as Noella released her legs.

Chapter Eleven

HARRIET LAY IN an exhausted heap on the bed as Edmund rolled off her after finally allowing himself to climax inside her still spasming body. For him, as well as her, it had been the most intense experience of his life. He looked at Lewis. 'Your turn tomorrow night,' he said with a faint smile.

Ella licked her lips in anticipation and smiled at Edmund. 'And mine with you,' she reminded him.

Edmund nodded, his eyes suddenly cool again. 'Indeed, tomorrow you and I spend the night together.'

Slowly Harriet sat up and looked about her. 'No,' she said clearly.

Edmund's eyes narrowed. 'What do you mean?'

'This is the end. The game's over.'

Lewis felt as though someone had hit him in

the stomach as the pain of her rejection struck home. 'Harriet, please . . .' he began.

'I know all I need to know now,' she continued, still keeping her gaze fixed on Edmund. 'This is the end.'

'But Lewis has to see how well he can do.'

'Tonight was for me, not for Lewis and most certainly not for you,' said Harriet calmly. 'I wanted to see how far it was possible for me to go and now I know.'

'But I satisfied you more than Lewis has ever done,' said Edmund. 'I know I did. Does this mean you're going to stay with me?'

She shook her head. 'Of course not.'

'Why?'

'Because I could never love you. You're a sexual technician, and a very good one, but there isn't anything more. That's probably enough for a lot of women, but not for me. I know now that for me sex alone isn't enough, however incredible. There has to be involvement, feeling, love if you like, otherwise it's pointless.'

'I do love you!' cried Edmund.

'No,' said Harriet, 'you only think you do. I'm not your kind of woman at all, except sexually.'

'Lewis doesn't love you,' said Edmund, his face twisting in rage. 'When we toasted tonight he toasted his film. I was the one who toasted you.'

Harriet looked at her husband and he stared back at her, his dark eyes full of pain. 'It's true,' he murmured. 'I don't know why. I wasn't thinking straight at the time.'

'It doesn't matter,' said Harriet quietly. 'I know how much the film means to you, and I'm sorry that I can't go on, but for me this is the end of the story.'

Lewis nodded. 'And for me. I knew even before you spoke that I couldn't make love to you in front of the others tomorrow night.'

'I think you're both mad!' exploded Edmund, grabbing hold of Ella's wrists and drawing her into the bathroom. 'I'm quite sure that there's still some pleasure to be had from the night's game even if you two won't join in. Perhaps it's Ella who's the true Helena.'

Noella slipped quietly away to join Oliver, knowing that she wouldn't return to America, and Lewis and Harriet found themselves alone.

'Did you mean what you said?' asked Harriet, as Lewis slipped her peignoir over her shoulders.

'About what?'

'About knowing you couldn't have gone on with the game tomorrow?'

'Yes. I was going to tell Edmund as soon as tonight was over.'

Harriet leant her head against his shoulder. 'Has this spoilt the film?'

'How could it? This *is* the end, and a very satisfying one as well.'

'There won't be any more films will there?' she asked later, when they'd returned to their own bed.

'Yes, but not involving us.'

'I'm glad. I knew you'd realise one day that there are some things that are more important than art.'

'And have you learnt anything as well?' he asked gently.

'Yes, that for me sex and love have to go together. Sheer sensation, however incredible, isn't enough. I'm glad I did what I did, but it's over now and I won't ever need to test myself again.'

'We need a proper holiday,' declared Lewis as they both turned on their sides and began to kiss. 'Where would you like to go?'

'Italy I think. I love opera and art, and I've had enough of Cornwall for the moment!'

Gently Lewis eased himself into her welcoming warmth and they began to move together in a blissfully familiar pattern. 'Italy it is, as long as you don't have a weakness for Italian men,' he laughed, watching her eyes widen as, to her incredulous delight, she felt her body coming alive again.

'Only half-Portuguese ones!' she promised him, closing her eyes as the warm glow began to fill her body.

To Lewis's horror, he suddenly had an image of his wife's fair-skinned body naked on a bed in the midday heat of Italy, her limbs entwined with the darker limbs of a young Italian male. It would make, he thought, as they both surged towards a climax, a very erotic shot.

In the next bedroom, almost out of her mind

with excitement, Ella was finally allowed to climax beneath Edmund's hands and tongue. Watching her panting with exhausted satisfaction, Edmund knew that at last he'd found his own, real life Helena.

And in the exercise room of the small cottage, Noella and Oliver toasted their future together.

Other bestselling X Libris titles available by mail: